I0517575

Young Studs

AN EROTIC SHORT STORY ANTHOLOGY

EMILY ROOKS

True Lust

YOUNG STUDS
AN EROTIC SHORT STORY ANTHOLOGY

Copyright Emily Rooks, 2025

A Production of True Lust

ISBN 978-1-948872-69-0

Manufactured in the United States of America
First printing February 2025

Contents

Bit of Pink

The clock behind the barista says I've been here a half-hour already, but I tell myself to remain patient, that he'll come in. He's been here alone two days in a row at the same time after all. Besides, I wore my red thong just for him. I pull out my compact mirror, check to see if I need to reapply my crème lipstick, a must for a woman of my age to look younger.

And then my stomach feels like it's going to flip, not because I can't make myself appear like I'm twentysomething but because I can't think of what to say to him should he come in. Keeping with a youthful mentality, I'd decided planning all of this out is somehow inauthentic and a betrayal of my self-confidence, but anyone with half a head knows that's stupid, and I realize I'm so out of practice.

The coffeeshop door swings open, a blinding rectangle of light, and from it he steps like he's a movie star... dirty blond hair neatly parted, striking gray eyes, swoonworthy dimples, tall with broad shoulders, a robust athletic build, like a hockey player. But there's something in his posture, a slight slump maybe, that shows something's wrong, that he's in need of care.

He passes me, and I steal a glance, as he orders coffee. Eight-ounce drip, black. The kind of coffee a young man down on his luck drinks – inexpensive, no frills. A few minutes later, he takes a seat in the far corner where there are no Christmas decorations, tosses his book bag on the chair across from him.

I occasionally glance his way, try to keep it infrequent, though that's difficult. Those sweet dimples of his are like a bottle of wine to an alcoholic. So I spend several minutes watching cars zoom up and down Independence Avenue and a bevy of bundled up college students speedwalking along the sidewalk, all for just a few seconds of glimpsing him.

Then my courage kicks in – maybe staring out the window with him nearby gave me time to get comfortable, to calm myself – and I decide to just keep looking at him, hoping he'll start looking at me. I don't, after all, have to say anything to get my message across.

My eyes lock onto him. He's staring off into space, as if he has all the time in the universe to do just that. His finger rubs the rim of his coffee cup. He takes a sip. Why doesn't he open his book bag and study?

And then he looks at me and three beats later toward his book bag. His gray eyes dart one way then the next, as he crosses then recrosses his legs. I keep staring at him. He glances my way again, and I flash him a smile. His mouth curls up – it's an automatic reflex – and once he realizes it, his face pinkens, and he looks away.

I won't stop staring, and just as his eyes turn back toward me, I bite my lip a little and, eyes filled with desire, look at him.

This time his gaze lingers on me. Maybe he's trying to

decide if he knows me from somewhere. Maybe he's wondering if I'm head over heels in love with him. Maybe he's questioning if I'm safe.

I'm not.

He smiles back then looks away again, trying not to be obvious. How sweet. I know he'll look back though. He's a guy. He has to. I hike up my skirt just enough that the next

time he does, he'll see what's underneath.

When he turns back to me, his eyes widen, as they go from my face to what's under the table. He can't stop staring.

And then I stand. The skirt falls where it should, and I pull on my jacket then head out the door, his eyes on me the entire time. I hope tonight he dreams of red thongs with a hand on his throbbing cock.

***

One year ago...

"Leandra, we need to talk."

I look up at Lindy, who's just arrived home. No *hello*, no *how was your day*, though both of those have been missing much of the past few years anyway. My chest tightens.

He gestures to the living room. I sit on the sofa, as he leans forward in his recliner.

"I don't quite know how to say this, so I'm just going to say it," Lindy says.

That's never good. I've heard those words hundreds of times on television shows and movies, and every time nothing good came out afterward.

3

"I want a divorce," he says.

My face pales. "What?"

"I want a divorce," he says matter-of-factly.

A thousand memories – of Maddy, our only child, playing on the living room floor between us, of the Halloween we turned the garage into a haunted house for the neighborhood kids, of Maddy opening the letter telling her she had a full-ride to an overseas college – flash through my head. How can one take away all of that?

As if reading my mind, he says, "You can have the house. The savings too. I want to make this amicable and give you what you deserve."

"I don't want to divorce," I say, emotionless, in shock.

"Leandra, you have to admit, neither of has been happy for a long time now."

"We can work through it. We can try marriage counseling, we can–"

He slowly shakes his head. "We can't."

My throat tightens. "Why not?"

"Because I'm in love with another woman, Leandra. A *younger* woman."

***

The barista doesn't seem to mind that I've come into the coffeeshop at the same time four days in a row. I myself am surprised that she's worked so many consecutive days.

What wouldn't surprise me is if he doesn't come in today. Part of me says that I've surely scared him off, but the other part of me says I've piqued his curiosity,

4

that he *wants* to return.

And sure enough, just like the past three days, he walks in at 1:35 p.m. He takes a long look at me, and I give him another smile, but he says nothing, just orders the eight-ounce drip, black, and returns to the corner seat. Our pieces are all back in place, we're ready to continue yesterday's chess match.

Time for the queen's gambit.

I stand up – and with coffee cup and my belongings in hand – walk straight toward his table, though I haven't got a clue what I'm going to say after my first line. "Mind if I join you?"

He seems to stumble over his words. "No – I mean yes, you can join me." He clumsily moves his book bag, almost knocking over his own coffee. The corner of my corner curls up.

I sit down, adjust my skirt. "I'm Leigh." Leandra sounds too old.

"Talon," he says.

Talon? Is he fucking shitting me? I suppose it's possible, a lot of my generation gave their kids stupid names, trying to be unique and clever and all of that. Well, if it isn't really his name, that's fine. I think it's kinda cool sounding in all truth.

"You're a student at KCU, Talon?" I kinda like how his name rolls of my tongue.

He nods. "You too?"

I shake my head. "I just like the coffee here."

"Um, I've noticed you've come in here four days straight now."

What do you know, I'm not day-old bread; I've still got some appeal left in me. I feel flattered and, in all honesty, a little scared. "You've very observant. I like an observant man."

"I appreciate you coming over here to talk."

"Oh? And why's that?"

"I broke up with my girlfriend a couple of weeks ago. I've been a little gun shy with women since then."

Mhm, I could be his rebound. *Perfect.* No attachments, just a good long night of fucking, exactly what we both need. "That explains your slump when you walk."

His eyebrows go up. "I'm slumping when I walk?"

"Just a little. Don't worry, you still look very handsome."

His mouth crinkles, as he looks down for a moment. "Look Leigh, just to be clear, I'm not interested in a relationship."

Because I'm old enough to be your mom or because it's too soon after your breakup?

"But I'm happy to converse," he quick adds.

Looks like I need to find out. But how? "I'd like to talk too. What caused your breakup?"

His face pales. "Um...we had a difference of...opinion."

I nod. He's hiding something. Then it comes to me how to find out about why he's not interested in a relationship. "Sorry, but I really need to go." I stand up. "Maybe another time?"

His shoulders slump, as his gray eyes dull. *That's a good sign.* "Sure," he says.

I throw on my jacket, sling the purse over a shoulder

6

and head to the bathroom. Once there, I take a deep breath, then bend down slightly and slip off my black lace panties. I crumple them into a tight ball that remains hidden in my hand.

On my way out of the coffeeshop, I stop in front of him. I knew he'd stay – he had to, if only to see if I'd change my mind about leaving.

"Hold out your hand," I say.

He hesitates at first and stares into my face, then brings his palm outward. I place my balled up panties in it then my fingers press his hand into a fist around the fabric.

"Return those to me tomorrow," I say and walk out.

A smile covers my face. I hope he cums into my black lace panties tonight.

***

Six months ago...

The house is emptier without Lindy and Maddy around, despite that neither took much with them. I can't decide if I wish they had or not. The absence of Lindy's recliner and Maddy's chess set on the mantel would remind me of them just as much as they now do by being there.

Not that I haven't felt emptiness during the past few years of marriage.

Maybe he'll come to his senses, I sometimes tell myself. This younger woman is just a fling; I can be younger myself again, especially now that Maddy is off to college.

But then I ask myself why I would want to be with a

man who cheated on me. Perhaps because my life with him is the only one I've known for the past twenty years? Am I afraid of the future?

Did he mean to be cruel when he gave me our home? Did he know there would be a thousand reminders in it of the unhappiness he got to leave behind?

I slowly sit on the sofa, and another stomach ache strikes. Everything I've ever loved is gone, and this home is just a reminder of that. For years, I've been slowly disappearing from their lives, from myself. And now I am just a ghost in this house.

***

There's a new barista working on day five. She tries to push the new snowmen sugar cookies on me. They *are* nicely decorated. But my waist needs to remain thin, just like it was back in college.

With Talon, I decide to up the ante and sit at his table in the far corner. There's a good view of the whole establishment from it; I can see why he likes sitting here.

A blinding rectangular light appears in the coffeehouse wall, as he steps through the door. He looks at where I used to sit then back at his corner seat, sees me. I flash him a smile.

He nods, gets his coffee. Guess he didn't mind me handing him my panties.

Yet, now that the moment of our meeting has come, my stomach aches again. What would a young man see in a middle-aged woman? I'm not smooth-skinned or a size four. I carry emotional bruises. He shouldn't expect children from me, not at my age. Ultimately, he'll have to spend decades of his life without me once I pass into the undiscovered country.

As he approaches, I straighten myself. This isn't about spending forever together or even about him, I tell myself. No, this is about me healing.

"Hello," he says, a little tremble in his voice.

"Hello yourself. I'm glad you came back."

His brow furrows a little. "Well, I had to find out something."

My eyebrows rise in anticipation of his question. God, his dimples are beautiful.

"Charity didn't ask you to do this, did she?"

"Charity?"

"My ex-girlfriend."

I chuckle. "No, not at all. Is she the kind who would do something like that?"

"Not really, though she could be an old hag sometimes. But, well–"

"Hell hath no fury like a woman scorned."

His mouth parts as he leans back. "I didn't say that. Besides, she broke up with me."

"Women only break up because they feel scorned."

His head tilts slightly as he gazes into the distance. "I guess I could see that..."

"So you're wondering why I'm talking to you, why I gave you my panties yesterday."

"Yeah."

"I'm talking to you because I find you quite handsome." His face pinkens. "I gave you my panties because...well, because I find you *very* handsome."

"You're not with anyone?"

Mhm, is he asking that because an older woman by my age should be married? Or is there another reason? "Why?"

"Because I find you very attractive too. I'm surprised someone like you *isn't* with someone else."

"I think that's the nicest thing anyone has said to me in a long time. No, I'm not with anyone."

We silently stare into one another's eyes for a few seconds too long. Hmm, could I train him to fuck me, just the way I like to be?

"My panties?" I say. "You were to bring them back to me today."

His face blushes, then a few seconds later he unzips his backpack and pulls a wadded black ball out – I wonder if his cum is still on it – and discretely hands it to me. The ball is soft, dry.

"Did you..."

His face turns crimson, making his gray eyes stand out even more. "Did I what?"

I grin mischievously. "Did you masturbate with them?"

He shakes his head slowly.

My gaze drops, as I frown. "Oh. I thought–"

His voice turns meek, as his muscles seem to tighten. "Please don't judge me, but... well, I *wore* them. I wore your panties."

***

Three months ago...

10

I pick up a framed photo of Lindy and me from our college days, arms wrapped around one another's shoulders, wearing red university sweatshirts, our smiles bright, the future an endless horizon of possibility. I remember that and all of our other days from then so well.

Like that day I was late so started running to class and like a goof tripped over my feet. His hand caught my waist and stopped my fall. He was so strong yet gentle. I smiled gratefully at him then hurried off to class.

Two days later, as we passed again on that same sidewalk, he asked me out to coffee.

We were known as "The L's" and while not a power couple we certainly were a cute one, known to all.

"Why me?" he used to ask. "You can have any man you want."

I knew that wasn't true or I would have dated my high school's starting quarterback with the killer dimples or our college's muscular, star hockey player. But I didn't really want them anyway. I wanted *him*.

And I proved it to him, and he proved his desire for me. I wasn't just a bit of pink to him. We had sex nearly every day, trying any position we could think of and sometimes even a little light bondage.

I wish I could go back to those wild, carefree days.

But all we have is today, this lone moment in the present.

And in this moment, I realize, just like then, I can be whoever I want to be. I can even be young again.

***

I lean back as my eyebrows rise. "Ohhh..."

The must be why Talon broke up with his girlfriend. For a moment, I imagine my muscular young stud donning her panties without her knowing about it. I find myself, surprisingly, growing tingly between the legs.

"Did you enjoy...wearing them?"

He nods. The red on his face dims.

"Would you like to try on another of my panties?" Where the hell did that thought come from?

He nods again, more slowly this time.

"Then you'll need to come home with me."

"Come home with you?"

"It will be entirely safe, Talon. I live alone, and I won't judge you. In fact, I'm a little...*fascinated* by it."

The tension leaves his brow. "But why do we have to go to your house?"

"Because my sweet young man, right now I'm *not* wearing any panties."

***

One month ago...

I position the new painting on its nails, replacing the one Lindy and I had bought of a mountain with a stream of meltwater flowing off it into a valley. As standing back, I admired the rhythms in the artist's brushstrokes, how the admiral blue color draws attention to the abstract paper-white face.

The colors remind me of a poster I saw in a guy's dorm room back in college, from before I met Lindy. I don't remember the guy's name – we both were drunk on alcohol and hormones – and maybe he didn't even tell me it.

I *do* remember shrieking when he flips me onto my stomach, raises my hips, and enters me. I spread my knees wider to accommodate him.

He wraps a hand around my throat, squeezing lightly. "Harder!" I manage to get out.

I struggle to suck in air, as he thrusts into me at furious pace. Then his cock finds that spot deep inside me. Black spots color my vision as I orgasm.

As I recall the thrill of that night, the space between my legs grows damp.

Wow, I need a man now just as much as I need a new painting.

No, I need a man to please me as I want to be pleased...even if I have to train him.

***

The entire drive to my place, I feel like he should be sitting in the back rather than the passenger seat. We make small talk – his major, what I do for a job, names of our hometowns – and that helps assure me that I'm not bringing home a serial killer. Funny that I never worried about that in college.

Once inside, Talon gawks at the furniture and appliances, probably wonders where the Christmas decorations are – as he follows me like a puppy to the bedroom. I still wonder if he cares or not that I am older than him but decide rather than facing the issue, I'll just entice him.

So I open the drawer with my undergarments in it. "Is there a kind of panties you prefer to wear?"

He peeks at the drawer, trying to be discrete about it. "Charity usually wore slips."

"So my black lace panties were the first you wore other than slips?"

He nods.

I find it strangely flattering. "I'm sure we can do better than slips. Here, take a look at these." I pull out an emerald green string and a candy pink Brazilian. "Maybe one of these interest you."

His eyes go to the string panties, but he doesn't say anything.

"I see you like the emerald green. Get undressed so you can try them on." A surge of power and lust rises through me. I wonder if this was what a man feels like when ordering his drunken girlfriend to get naked.

Talon pulls his sweater over his dirty blond hair, leaving it slightly ruffled. He's not wearing a shirt beneath it, and I wasn't wrong about his athletic build – he's got firm pecs and six-pack abs. When he leans down to slip off his shoes and socks, the muscles in his arms flex. His pants drop to the carpet, and his hard-on already is apparent under his boxers, which he shimmies down his legs until he's entirely naked. His cock stands straight out, a thick ivory pole.

He slips the green string over his feet and brings it up his muscular calves and thighs. His bulging cock strains against the thin line of fabric, and his balls hang out of the string's sides. Hmm, looks like a Christmas decoration to me.

"How does that feel?" I ask.

"It's kind of...exciting."

"It does look sexy on you."

His pretty gray eyes light up at that. "It does?"

I nodded. "Very much. So why did you try on Charity's panties?"

"I was just curious."

"You'll find I'm fairly open about such things." Then I got real close to him, right into his face. "In fact, perhaps today I should be 'the man.' Is that okay with you?"

He nods, a slight grin on his face.

I step past him and slap his butt real quick. "Excellent. I'll be right back – and when I am, I expect you to be in those pink Brazilians."

Heading into the bathroom, I quick wash my privates and without a stitch of clothes on add some lipstick to my mouth. *Me* be the man? Who am I kidding? He might be wearing my panties right now, but I'm primping myself to *be* fucked good and hard.

Then a thought crosses my mind – what if he's not into women? Maybe this Charity was a cover for his homosexuality. I'm cool if that's the case, but it also means I am in for a another night with Tickle Kitty.

No, I decide, he likes women. He just has a panties fetish, and it is as huge of a turn-on for me as it is for him. I pucker my lips to get the pink coloring even. Looking at my curves and full breasts in the mirror, a smile forms on my face. He makes me feel young and free. I can be silly with him, play this role reversal game.

My ex-husband wouldn't do that. After all, a mother doesn't play games like this.

15

***

One week ago...

The better part of a month spent redecorating and scrolling through dating sites has left me gloomy. Furniture bought with Lindy, color patterns we agreed on...profiles of balding men, pictures of them with their smiling, grown daughters...there's no escaping my age.

I find myself looking more and more at the younger men on the sites. They're often short on words, but what few they do use tend to be full of spunk. Their pictures interest me the most – vibrant and fresh faces and heads full of hair, the festive places they've gone. Despite saying they want to form a deep, emotional bond, their pictures betray them...they clearly just want sex with willing women.

Looking at my laptop's clock, I wince. For the last half-hour, I've focused on just one muscular young man's profile, staring at each of his photos, almost all of them taken at his university.

Shutting down the laptop, I head into the bedroom, pull my Tickle Kitty from the nightstand drawer. I imagine that young stud positioning himself atop him, rubbing his cockhead against my wet slit. As he enters me in my mind, my vibrator goes on in the real world, and I moan. The slaps of our body against one another and my gasps fill the room, as my body shakes with the suction of my clit. His fingers press just below my jaw. A moment later, my body goes rigid, as I scream out my orgasm, then I float on a current of warm air, slowly drifting back to the mattress.

When I do land, I imagine him saying, "Let's go again."
Okay, I need to find a young buck to fuck.

***

I step into the bedroom. His eyes widen then narrow, burning with lust. Yeah, he likes women.

And what a sight he is to see. His cockhead sticks out the top of the pink panties that press tight around his pole; his hairy testicles stick out of both leg holes.

I pirouette around him, so my back is to his front. Shimmying against his body, I take his hands and bring them to my front so his arms are wrapped about my tummy. The silkiness of my pink panties and the rock hardness of his cock press against my ass.

"Kiss my neck," I tell him. "Work your way down it to my breasts."

His warm lips graze my skin just below my ear, and my eyes instantly close, as I let go a gasp of pleasure. Electricity flows through my neck, as he slowly closes on my shoulder. I grind back on him.

He shifts, still keeping me wrapped in his arms, so he can reach my breasts. His lips nip their tops, then focuses on one, circling around it with kisses, spiraling in on my nipple, until the tip of his tongue flicks it.

"Throw me on the bed," I whisper huskily. "Make me cum with your tongue."

He squats, places one arm below my knees and lifts me off the floor. A shriek of pleasure, like I'm on a carnival ride, escapes my mouth – I'm not heavy at all to him – and then his strong arms toss me onto the mattress. His hands grip my ankles, pulls me to the edge. He drops to his knees between my legs, pushes my thighs apart. His warm lips go to my pussy, then his tongue licks my clit, and my eyes close as I murmur in pleasure.

Yes, this is how I remember it. A young stud taking charge, proving that he is worthy enough to fuck me.

Except my young stud wears candy pink panties.

He pulls back, fingers my clit. My head spins, and I bring a hand to my breast, squeeze it, maybe to steady myself, maybe because I can't control myself.

Then his mouth goes back to my clit. His tongue is smooth, quick and agile, and I let go an "Ooooh," urging him on.

As his tongue performs its magic, his hands slide up my waist, and at my breasts tease and tweak my nipples. My mouth opens wide, lets go a gasp. With every swirl of his tongue, my muscles tense, and then as my whole body goes rigid, I scream. My mind is foggy, as a smile forms on my face, and I lick my lips.

That was fun.

***

Five days ago...

The university isn't far from my house. There's a coffeeshop almost bordering the campus, my map app says, and I find a parking space a block away. A garland of artificial spruce with red bows and tiny gold lights run across each wall. I order a coffee, take a seat by the window overlooking Independence Avenue.

Discretely, I assess the other college-aged men there. The slender one with a goatee has his head buried in a book. Another one looks a little more fit but wears his sports cap backwards, like that makes him cool or something. A handsome one with the most beautiful eyelashes sits across from an equally delightful-looking girl, as they converse. Hmm, not a lot here. Maybe I ought to be home decorating for a Christmas that no one will be at.

Am I being too picky? Back in college, I once slept with a guy who looks like Mr. Sports Cap. One evening I went over to his dorm room, and we watched a movie; I didn't think it would go further than that. He had good hands, though. I recall being self-conscious about undressing because I was wearing royal blue boybriefs. He didn't seem to mind, but then his attention was more on my full breasts than anything else when he undressed me.

I glance up at the clock behind the baked goods case. 1:35. I wonder if I just came at a bad time and should try earlier in the day.

And then there's a blinding flash from the coffeeshop door opening. A tall albeit slumping man with broad shoulders walks in. As the door closes, his silhouette gains color and texture. He's young and has the sexiest dimples I've ever seen.

The twentysomething pays me no attention, orders an eight-ounce drip, black, and takes a seat in the far corner. He tosses his book bag in the chair across the table from him. I surf the net on my phone, stealing glances every few minutes at him, trying to see his eyes. They are gray. I wonder if that's their real color or if it's because he feels gloomy.

Hmm, how to talk to him?

I look back at my phone, nurse my now cold coffee.

And then, the next time I glance up, he's slinging his book bag over a shoulder and heading through the door. His pert ass is the last I see of him, as he disappears into the brightness and the door closes behind him.

I sigh. Tonight, my Tickle Kitty will be his tongue.

***

Talon rises from his kneeling position, tugs the pink panties to below his testicles. His erect cock bobs. He's no longer slumping.

I sit up, bring my palm to his chest. "Remember, I'm the man?"

He nods though his brow furrows.

"Lay down on the bed."

He gets on it, his head atop a pillow. Moving on my knees, I scoot between his legs, grip his cock.

"Pull your knees to your chest."

As he does, I hold his cock so it sticks out from between his thighs, pointing toward me. A bit of pink fabric is visible beneath his balls. Standing on the bed, I stare down at him, a mischievous smile on my face, and squat.

I'd always wanted to try this position with Lindy. Somehow over the years we got satisfied with only doing it missionary style.

Once my wet lips meet the thick head of his cock, my eyes involuntarily close with pleasure, and I moan as my pussy slides down onto it.

Rising a little, I drop myself fully onto his cock, and he moans. I rise and drop again, this time faster, and keep it up until his hips thrust upward, sending his cock into me. My hands grip his ankles to steady myself, as my breathing deepens.

He's mine to have, and I grind down on him, like I'm doing a belly dance. He moans every time I take him in and growls in pleasure as my pussy lips reach where his cock rises from his groin. Excited by his reaction, my speed picks up, and his moans grow louder.

"Choke me," I somehow get out between gasps.

He hesitates then his hand comes up between his raised legs and wraps itself around my throat. He is gentle, doesn't want to hurt me, but soon he won't be able to stop himself.

With each of my thrusts, I sense his muscles tensing, then his free hand runs along my calf and grips it, holding on for the inevitable explosion. My eyes close, and I bite my lower lip.

Then his hands tighten around my calf and throat as he roars, and his hot seed shoots up inside me. An instant later, my body tenses, and then there it is again, that incredible wave of pleasure as my mind sees nothing but mist around me.

***

Four days ago...

I arrive at 1:20, take the same seat as the previous day. My hand brushes off a piece of lint that somehow has stuck itself to my jeans, and I wait.

Just in case he doesn't show, I peruse the other

college-aged men there as alternatives. One with curly hair and thin eyes wears a purple KCU sweatshirt with its distinctive snake wound around a staff logo on it. A beefy man with close-cropped black hair and gold wire-rim glasses rubs his eyes then goes back to reading his thick textbook. Beautiful eyelashes and his pretty girl are back, sitting side by side on the sofa, making googly eyes at one another, his hand on her bare knee that is closest to him.

Then at 1:35, like clockwork, my gray-eyed hunk walks in. He orders coffee, still is slumping, and takes the same seat as the day before. I wonder if everyone has assigned seats at the coffeeshop. Hmm, maybe that would be a good opening line to start a conversation with him.

No, that's a stupid idea.

Just walk over and introduce yourself. "Hi, I'm Leandra. May I sit here please?"

No, that sounds stupid too.

I scroll through my phone, not really paying attention to any of the pics or text on the screen, unable to think of anything to say. Glancing up, what catches my attention isn't him, though, but pretty girl. She's taken beautiful eyelashes' hand and slowly drags it up her thigh to beneath her skirt.

Then it strikes me – I know exactly how to get him interested in me, and I won't have to say anything at all.

But my plan will have to wait until tomorrow.

***

Once his cock goes to half-mast, I fall back onto my

ass, still dizzy.

"Give me a second," he says, his voice breathy.

My brow furrows. "A second for what?"

He sits up, slowly. "We're going to do it again."

My eyes brighten. "Really?"

He nods. "While I catch my breath, get me ready."

I get on all fours between his legs and twirled my tongue around his shaft as gently cupping his balls. His pole rises and thickens again, and I bring it to full mast by slowly moving my mouth back and forth over it. My tongue catches the salty taste of his cum.

"Lay back," he says.

I do, and sitting up on his knees, he grips my ankles, raising them into the air so they are above his shoulders. His cock slides into me.

I moan in approval and close my eyes.

With each thrust, his speed picks up a notch, until he's jackhammering me, giving me a proper fucking. I look up at him, see my pink Brazilians still wrapped around his thighs, and the excitement of seeing it provides the perfect lubricant, as he continues to fuck me with abandon.

His grunts grow louder, as do my moans, creating a symphony of sounds as our skin, lathered in one another's sweat, slap against one another.

Then his cock pulses in my pussy, and his hands grip my ankles tight, as he makes one last slam into me and roars. He shudders, and ropes of his warm cum pour into me.

Then I buck against him, and gasp as entering that

land of fog and mist. *Holy fuck, that's just what I needed.*

***

Talon holds my legs until his cock softens and slips out of my pussy. He collapses back onto the bed.

Somehow I crawl up next to his young, muscular body, and curl next to him, as he stretches his legs and snakes an arm around my shoulder.

Our breathing and heartbeats calm after a few minutes.

"I'm sorry," he says, "I think I got cum on your panties."

I giggle. "That's quite all right."

"And I have one more confession to make."

I'm almost too tired to care. "What's that?" I murmur.

"I also prefer older women. Women in their forties like you."

Now I'm awake. "Oh?"

"Charity was 41."

I have a year on her in age. "Sounds like I'll have to go shopping for more panties tomorrow."

Talon chuckles, as his hand caresses my back, and I relax, like a cat curled up in a lap. No matter what our age, all we have is today and this very moment, and for the first time in a long while, I'm relishing it. I'm with a man who makes me smile, who makes me feel alive.

Isn't that what's most important?

Star Pupil

What do single teachers do on weekends? As placing a carton of ice cream in my grocery cart on yet another Friday night, I wished I would have thought of that back in college. Somehow all of my colleagues and old friends were married, so that meant I pretty much was an expert on Netflix's entire catalog and had the cleanest apartment in town.

It's not like I was bad looking or anything. I had the classic hourglass figure, long silky hair, high eyebrows, a small nose, and when in my tight jade dress I could make any man turn around and stare at me. Not bad for a 30-year-old.

But there just weren't a lot of single guys to choose from in McCulloch, Texas, and the ones available preferred to spend their weekends at Kelly's Tavern or were old enough to be my grandfather. Not that it mattered anyway; I'd broken up several months ago with my boyfriend who after we'd moved in together never paid me an iota of attention, so I'd been reluctant to get back into the game. Still, on weekends that May, I felt adrift, cast into an ocean until the currents brought me back to Monday morning's classroom.

"Miss Kirill?"

The voice sounded familiar, and I turned around. My

eyes instantly widened. "Prentice?" Oh my God, Prentice from my student teaching days.

"I'm surprised that you remember me."

How could I not? His puppy love crush on me was cute as hell. He was no puppy now, though, had filled out with broad shoulders and muscular chest, sported a full head of chestnut brown hair that was nicely cut, offered a boyish grin, and spoke in a deep voice. He was far from the nerdy, awkward seventh grader who stared all hour at me.

"I'm surprised that *you* remember *me*," I said. "I was only there for a semester."

"Oh, I'd never forget you. But since you remember me, guess I should apologize for not being the best student."

I smiled. "You were always very attentive."

We just stood there for a long moment, then he burst out, "Wow, you look good, Miss Kirill." His face turned a shade of red. "I'm sorry, I didn't mean – you've just aged well." The red deepened. "I'm sorry, I keep putting my foot in my–"

"It's okay," I interrupted, as suppressing a chuckle. He still had it for me. "You must be going to college this fall?" Wait, how did I just know that? I teach English not math; I can't add and subtract numbers that fast.

He nodded. "Just graduated last week. Going to Southwest State in fall. Engineering."

Hmm, smart as well good looking. Too bad he wasn't my age.

"What about you? Still teaching?"

My turn to nod. "At East." His crosstown rival.

"It's too bad you didn't land a job at Central."

"It is. Watching you mature into a young man would have been wonderful." *Did I just say that?* I think my face blushed. Teachers quickly learn how to recompose themselves when messing up in front of 30 students, though, and I too recovered. "It's Friday night." I glanced around. "Where are your friends?" *Where is your girlfriend?*

He looked down for a second. "Everyone is out on a date. Looks like it's YouTube for me tonight."

Ah, a kindred spirit. Maybe it didn't matter that he wasn't my age. "I have Netflix."

"Cool. My parents are too cheap for it. Saving for my college education, I guess. I've always wanted to see *Adams Falls.*"

He didn't get the hint. A typical male for his age, he still had a lot to learn. "Great series. I'd be happy to let you watch it at my place."

Prentice blinked in surprise. "Yeah, I'd love that."

Definitely slow on the uptake. I could teach him a lot. "I'm not doing anything tonight." *Yeah, and I'm not doing anything tomorrow night or next weekend either.* "You spring for the snacks, and you're welcome to come over."

He peered at me with furrowed brows then his green eyes brightened. "Okay – yeah, sure. That would be awesome, Miss Kirill."

I wanted to tell him to call me *Anjelica* but somehow found him calling me "Miss Kirill" appropriate – *I am the master, after all, and he should treat me with respect.* So I moved the ice cream from my cart to his. "I'll meet you out front after you check out."

***

We watched *Adams Falls* and enjoyed the snacks, as sitting apart on my couch. When the episode ended, he ran his hands up and down his black jeans.

"Thanks for letting me watch the show," he said. "I'm hooked. It's a fantastic show –characters you can identify with and root for, a fast-moving plot that pushes the limits of what's acceptable, interesting metaphors commenting on contemporary issues."

I grinned. "That's well thought out. Looks like you remember how to organize your thoughts with a topic sentence and three supporting points."

"Learned it in your class. You always were a great teacher. So patient, sticking with students until they got it."

That's for sure. I twirled my hair locks. "So all of your friends have dates. Why not you?"

His gaze fell to the floor. "Not very confident I guess."

I nodded. "You can't be afraid to look a girl in the eye. You must have dated some."

He shrugged. "A couple of girls here and there. Always with someone who didn't really want to date but just wanted to go out. Sitting at home gets boring, you know?"

Tell me about it. "Look Prentice, you're a handsome young man. Any number of girls would be happy to date you."

28

A smile slowly covered his face. "Handsome? You think so? Well of course you do, or you wouldn't have said it."

"And try not to overthink it. It makes you look indecisive, and girls don't like that." I ran a finger along his broad shoulder.

"They don't? No, they wouldn't. Why would they? Wait, I'm overthinking again, aren't I?"

I sniggered a little. "Yeah."

"Thank you for telling me. It's good to know. I'm not certain how I'll get along with girls in college given my inexperience. Any other advice, Miss Kirill?" If he were a puppy, I swear his big eyes would be staring at me while his tail barely contained an excited wag. *Maybe I shouldn't do this*, I told myself as biting my lip but then decided I wasn't spending another night alone, at least not this one anyway.

"Yes," I said, my finger still running along his shoulder. "When a woman touches you, that means she wants to be held."

His eyes widened slightly. I scooted closer to him, took his large hands, and gently pulled them and his arms around me. My body felt like it sank into a wagonload of cotton. *Mm-hmm, this boy has been working out.* We embraced, then pressed tighter into one another, and I caught a whiff of his citrus scent, clean and sharp. I felt his cock hardening against me; apparently he was filled out in all of his muscles.

I pulled away slightly, gazed straight at him. "Surely you've kissed some of those dates?"

A sadness seemed to fill his eyes, and he shook his head.

"Well, here's another lesson. Before you move in to kiss a woman, always lock eyes. This is a clear signal that you're thinking about kissing her. If she backs away or abruptly changes the topic, hold off on the kiss. Are you paying attention?"

He nodded.

"If she doesn't back away or change the subject, lean in slowly and pause for a second." I gently took his chin and guided it to match my instructions. "Bring your face closer to hers at a slow pace, so that she has plenty of time to back away. Tilt your head slightly, opposite of her tilt, otherwise your noses will be in the way. Stop just before you reach her lips. If she doesn't move, that probably means you can go ahead and kiss her. If she's really into you, she might even move in the last little bit and kiss you first. Now, let's see how well you were listening."

He remained still for what seemed like the longest second then did exactly as I had told him. When he paused just before reaching my lips, I moved in that last little bit.

We pulled apart, though just barely. "Now there's no need any more to stop before reaching her lips," I said. "You know she wants to kiss. Just keep your kisses light and soft...at first. This is particularly important if the two of you have never kissed before – you don't want to seem aggressive or unskilled. Okay, let's try it."

He tilted his head and moved in slowly, lightly

grazing his lips over mine, keeping the pressure as soft as possible. His lips were warm, tasted like chocolate with a hint of peppermint, and my heart fluttered. I wondered if his gentleness was more because of his tentativeness than because he was following my instructions, but as our lips separated, his strong hand stroked my waist. Good, he knew better than to just let his hands sit at his sides like limp noodles.

I drew back, had to catch my breath. "That was nice."

His face beamed, as a moment of silence passed between us.

I knew he wanted to go further. "Where do you want to touch me?" I said.

He hesitantly brought a hand toward my breast. My slender hand overlapped his and guided two of his fingertips in gentle circles above my nipple. Then my hand pressed his palm onto the breast's underside so that he cupped it while massaging. I closed my eyes, found myself floating away. With each deep and rhythmic breath, my nipples crested my blouse.

"Now the other one," I said.

His hand shifted to the neglected breast and repeated the massage and cupping. I shivered with pleasure. *Such a wonderful, attentive student.*

"Unbutton my blouse."

His fingers fumbled at my buttons, but eventually he got all of them. I held up my arms, motioning for him to pull off my sleeves, and he gently tugged at each hem, until the shirt slid off.

"Touch me again."

His large hands delicately caressed my bare shoulders, as if he were handling porcelain. Then his palms came to my breasts, and he repeated the circling of his fingers across them, only a thin layer of lace separating our skin. I closed my eyes, let out a soft sigh.

"Time for the bra to come off," I said and turned my back to him.

I felt his heated stare on my back for a long moment, apparently trying to figure out how this contraption came off. I thought of explaining it to him, but then decided if he was majoring in engineering, he'd figure it out.

After a couple of muddled attempts, he got it unlatched, and I turned to face him. My bra straps hung loose just above the elbows.

He leaned in and kissed the nape of my neck, and I swooned as his warm lips delicately worked their way across my skin. Then he pulled away and coaxed the bra off my arms and bosom.

At the sight of my bare breasts, he gasped.

Then he turned away, and without looking at me said, "There's something I must tell you. Back when you were a student teacher, I had the biggest crush on you, thought you were the most beautiful woman in the world. I fantasized a lot about you. I feel a little ashamed about it right now, and–"

I brought a finger to his lips. "Shhh. I know you did." His eyes and mouth widened. "But right now we're both adults, and I'm willing to let you live out your fantasy. You see, it's been a long time since I've been with a man, and you've...well, you've grown into *quite* a man."

The worry left his eyes.

"Would you like to continue?"

He nodded.

"Remember, slow and steady wins the race. A woman wants you to see her, to appreciate her."

His hands ran along my side, as if beholding something precious. Then his mouth came to a breast, and in a series of kisses he spiraled in on my nipple. When he arrived to it, his tongue flicked across the nub. I felt it harden and grow, as his lips pressed against then sucked it into his mouth. I swooned and grabbed the back of his head to steady myself then pressed his face into my bosom as caressing his hair. Pulling back from my breast, he went to the other one and repeated.

Dizzy from his attention and the heat in the air between us, I rose off the couch and pointed at my jeans. "Time for these to come off," I said, my voice low and husky.

He remained seated on the couch, slowly unsnapped the front and cautiously unzipped, as if afraid he might catch something in the teeth. Loosened from the waist, he inched the jeans down my thighs then past my calves. Once puddled on the floor, I stepped out of each leg.

One of his arms went around my lower back and another just below my butt check, as he planted soft kisses across my abdomen. I giggled half in delight and half because it tickled. His hand ran the length of my thigh, as he kissed to the top of my panties. A tiny wet

spot formed on its front, and he breathed in my musk.
Then his thumbs hooked into each side of the fabric, and
as he pulled downward, I shimmied them off.

His lips kissed my inner thighs then across the top of
my muff. I shivered as his hot breath drifted pass my
wet pussy.

"Stand up," I said.

He rose, his eyes searching, as if he'd something
wrong. I grabbed his hand to take him into the
bedroom, then after a step reached back and snatched
the ice cream off the coffee table. He gave me another
quizzical look, but I was off again, leading him along like
the puppy he was.

***

In the bedroom, I set the ice crem on the nightstand,
then opened the blinds just slightly. The moonlight cast
a dim blue
glow, leaving the room's corners in shadows.

"Come stand in front of the mirror," I said.

Once he did, I went behind him and slowly rolling his
T-shirt upward, letting my nails graze his skin along the
way. When the shirt reached his chest and could go no
farther, I pressed my breasts into his back and wrapped
my arms around his front so I could explore his taut abs.
He watched us in the mirror, and then I quick swiped
my nails across his abs. He simultaneously flinched in
surprise and moaned in pleasure.

I withdraw my hands to his sides. "Raise your arms."

When he did, I leisurely rolled his tee up over his
wide chest then his head and finally tugged them off his

EMILY ROOKS

arms.

"Hmmm, very nice," I said, as my hands caressed his chest then slid down to his abs. "Let's see what else you've got under those clothes."

My hands reached his belt and deftly unbuckled it. His breathing grew heavy, as he stood utterly still. *Such a well-behaved student.* My fingers undid his jean's snap then pulled down his zipper, a nail running down the length of his hard cock the entire way.

I slapped his behind. "Wiggle out of those for me."

He did, and then soon gravity took over and it was at his ankles. A moment later, he stepped out of them.

"And let's get rid of those socks too," I said.

He brought a knee up and bent slightly to pull it off, as my hands glided across his thick thighs, then he did the same with the other foot.

That left him with just one article remaining, but I wanted to make sure he knew that we had a ways to go. I caressed his pert ass cheeks through his briefs, then cupped each one and squeezed. My fingers worked their way to his front, ran along each side of his cock up to its mushroom head. I rubbed the underside of his member just below the head, and his neck arched back as he moaned.

Hooking my fingers into the sides of his waistband, I unhurriedly rolled the briefs downward over the summit of his ass' curve then bending down took it past his thighs and knees until they too could fall. He stepped out of them as well, as I rose, skimming his skin with my nails. Once standing, I looked over his shoulder at him the mirror.

I gasped.

His cock was as big as a cucumber in both girth and length. I had never seen one that large before. *Looks like he might teach me something tonight.*

***

I stepped off to the side to take him all in. His toned muscles rippled beneath his tanned skin. His long, beautiful cock stood fully erect, its head glistening with precum. I didn't know if I could take that monster inside me, but I wasn't going to tell him that. You never discourage student after all.

Besides, we had a long way to go before I needed to worry about his cock.

"Lay down on the bed," I said.

When he did, I got up onto the mattress, sat on my knees next to his torso, and dipped a finger into the ice cream. Hovering above his navel, I turned my finger over, let the chocolate splat onto his tummy.

Prentice jerked at first from the cold, but as the ice cream slid slowly down his abs, I leaned down and with my warm tongue lapped it off his skin. He shivered in pleasure at the sudden change in temperature.

I ran my finger through the ice cream again, dropped the dollop above his right nipple, slurped it off again. He squirmed and moaned. The chocolate and marshmallow flavor mixed well with the saltiness of his sweat.

Then I did it again but to his right rib. Then his left thigh. His right shoulder. Above his left nipple. His strong hands caressed my sides. Then a dollop on his neck. My lips ran up the length of his throat, over his chin, and to his mouth, and we kissed deeply. Our tongues entwined, as I shared with him the chocolate on my tongue.

"My turn," I said, as pulling away and laying down on the bed. He took the ice cream container from me, and repeated my dip and drip, letting the first dollop and his warm mouth fall on my abdomen. Then my right breast. Left thigh. The crevice between my shoulders and neck. My right thigh. Left nipple. The hair just above my pussy. Each time, I shivered with more wild abandon.

I sat up, took the ice cream container from him and placed it on the bedstand. He watched me, his cock fully primed, its bloated head looking like a small boxing glove. *Time to train the fighter.*

"That was wonderful," I said. "Now, here's an important lesson for you to take to heart: Always take your time pleasing a woman; make it a priority over your own pleasure. She'll reward you afterward in ways that are much more spectacular than if you take the wham-bam-thank-you-ma'am approach. And she'll come back for more – as well as tell all of her friends, and you can bet that some of them will suddenly be quite interested in you."

His mouth fell slightly open at that, as if it were a stunning revelation, like a caveman seeing a wheel in action for the first time.

"Now, to help you learn to take your time, I want you lick my pussy until I orgasm." I reclined on the bed.

His eyes widened.

"Trust me, if you can make me cum, I'll please you like you've never been pleased before."

He slid down to between my legs then his tongue run in a long lap along my slit. Wetted, it parted easily for him. His tongue found my vaginal opening and focused on that. Ah, young men, always interested in a gal's anatomy but entirely clueless about it. My hand went to back of his head, guided it my clit.

My neck arched back as a wave of tingles cascaded through me. "Yes, right there," I gasped.

His tongue slid up and down over my clit. Instantly my eyes closed, and the warmth of his breath upon my most private parts sent my heart rate rising. I found myself drifting away from the world of all my problems.

I ran my fingers through his hair. "Just a little bit slower, baby."

His tongue downshifted as he switched to broader, circular movements around my clit.

My breathing deepened, and I let out small whimpers of pleasure. "Yeah...yeah...that feels so good," I moaned.

His hand slid along my tummy to a breast. He cupped and squeezed it then let his finger play with my nipple while his tongue worked over my clit. My pussy grew damp, as I gasped. *Ah, a man who can do two things at once – he's moving to the head of the class!*

My hips slowly gyrated to his tongue, and that must have excited him, for his tongue worked my clit just a little but faster. As my gyrations rose in speed, so did his laps around my happy button, first going clockwise then counter-clockwise, then clockwise again and alternating until I didn't know where his tongue was anymore, just knew that I didn't want him to stop.

I wanted to surrender, spread my legs, move Prentice's hips between them, let him fuck me to ecstasy. *No,* I told myself, *first he has to make me cum with his tongue. He must master this lesson before moving to the next level.*

My back arched, as my nails dug into his head, and I let out a loud moan. Sublime waves of pleasure washed over my body. *God, I can't wait for him to be inside me.*

***

At last, I opened my eyes and gazed at him in anticipation.

He sat on his knees in front of me, as if a knight before his queen, his hard-on piercing the space between us. But he did not move.

"You need to be assertive, show confidence," I said, though given his size I wondered if the pep talk was meant for me. "Confidence is a turn-on. I know you want to do it, and if a woman is under you in this position not struggling, she wants to do it too. So you need to do it – or I'll start to wonder if you really want to, and then if I get self-conscious I may not want to anymore."

He grinned. "Isn't that overthinking it?" The tip of his cock breached my pussy lips.

I giggled. "Yeah, I am. Now keep sliding it in, just a little at a time, let me get used to you. Every woman needs a few seconds to get used to a man being there, but with your size, it may take a little longer."

That seemed to give him confidence because he did

exactly as he was told until his cock was buried deep inside me. My head spun dizzily, as every nerve in my pussy fired.

I wrapped my arms around his back, caressed the back of his head. "Now fuck me."

He didn't hesitate. His hips undulated, as he thrust in and out. His chest rose and fell faster than before, as my breathing grew ragged. Within a few seconds, his eyes fluttered, and he let out a deep moan, cumming inside me. Ah, how could I forget that these young men have no staying power? His weight collapsed down on me, and I caressed the back of his head, as his panting gradually eased.

Finally, he seemed to regather his strength and began to rise off me. My arms pressed tight against him, holding him in place. "Where do you think you're going?"

"Well, I—"

"You came fast." Even in the dim light I could see his face redden slightly. "It's okay. Young men are that way. But if you cum fast, you aren't done. A lady expects more. She deserves more. After you've rested a moment or two, you need to find the inner will to keep going."

"Keep going? I don't think I have anything left—"

"You do," I interrupted. "And if you keep going, a woman will help ensure you'll keep drawing on that inner strength."

He looked at me a bit oddly but started moving his hips again. I squeezed my vagina muscles to ensure his cock remained hard. After my first couple of light moans, he fell into a steady rhythm of thrusting in and out of me.

"That feels good," I said, raising my knees until the heels of my feet pressed against his buttocks.

His own moans lengthened and breathing deepened. He was a sight to behold as he fucked me. With each thrust, his biceps tightened and loosened, and his expression was a strange mixture of pleasure and pain, as our bodies, oiled in sweat, slid against one another. *My star pupil.*

After a few minutes, he lifted himself and extended his arms so that our torsos no longer touched. "Stay like that," I said, as reaching a finger to my clit and gently rubbing it from side to side.

With his thrusts and groans, my finger moved faster and pressed harder. Every muscle in my body tensed, and I pressed even more as approaching the edge. His strokes grew longer, deeper, more forceful. Grunting and groaning, he panted, "Oh Miss Kirill...Miss Kirill." His muscles rippled like cables beneath his skin, and rivulets of sweat ran along his arms, as he rammed in and out of me.

He thrust his hips forward harder than before and growled, as his cum gushed deep inside me. I stiffened then bucked and arched up as letting go a low groan. A tiny spot of beautiful, white light – warm, beautiful, welcoming – enveloped me.

He deserves an A.

After several seconds, he rolled off me, collapsed onto his back. I snuggled against him, using his chest as a pillow, as he stroked my hair. My pussy ached from his size, but somehow in the afterglow that felt all right, like the burn in your legs when you have runner's high.

"There are more episodes of *Adams Falls* to watch," he said. "I'll be over tomorrow night to watch the next one."

Excellent, he was learning. "That would be fun," I said. "I have many more lessons to impart."

And finally something to do on weekends.

Players

"You're pretty damn good to keep up!"

I glanced at the two guys who kept playing frisbee in front of us girls, obviously trying to impress. Being the first day of summer, they didn't waste any time. Not that we minded. They definitely were eye candy.

"I didn't think you were this slow," the sexier of the two guys shouted back to his buddy. He whipped the frisbee, and it sailed, a red disk across the clear blue sky.

His buddy plucked it from the air then flicked the disk back. The wind off the bay caught it, and after floating on an air current the frisbee landed at my bare feet, shooting up a little sand.

The sexy guy ran up to me, grabbed the frisbee. "Sorry about that," he said, his shaggy blond hair flopping over his forehead.

I smiled. "It's all right."

He smiled back, locking his eyes for a few seconds on mine, then took off for the open beach, and I watched his tanned, muscled body run. He snapped his wrist, and the frisbee floated into the air back to his buddy – whose head it flew over, forcing him to chase after it before the waves pulled it out to the water.

The sexy one glanced my way. Surely he knew I'd been staring at him. While his buddy ran after the red disk rolling on the wet sand, he came over to me.

"Hey, sorry again about that. I'm Brandon." His eyes scanned my body.

"Taylor," I said.

"You've got the prettiest green eyes, Taylor."

And your ice blue eyes are damn hot themselves. I smiled. "Thank you. Great first day, uh?"

He nodded. "Will you be hanging around a while?"

"Probably."

"Cool. When Randy gets tired of frisbee, I'll look for you."

I giggled. "Sure."

Brandon moved along the shore to find Randy, who looked like he was halfway down the beach.

"You certainly made that easy," my friend Ariana said from the beach towel next to mine.

"How's that?"

"You basically said you'd wait for him."

"What's wrong with that?"

"Make him work for it, girl."

"Who said I won't?"

Elle, the chubby one in our trio, sat up on the other side of me. "Ah, the old hook, line and sinker. Nice move, Taylor."

"I hear he's another Central High player," Ariana said, "so it's more like Taylor is on his hook."

Ariana laid back down, then so did Elle and me, soaking in the sun. We were finally free, enjoying that first day of summer between high school graduation and college. There were days that past spring I was so bored that I never thought we'd get this far; West High felt like a prison sentence that never would end. But now we had a summer off, to do whatever.

"Yeah, but girls," I said, "did you see his firm butt?"

***

After a couple of hours of laying in the sun, I sat up. The thick layer of coconut-scented sunscreen had sweated off, and I applied more. The morning felt like it was lasting forever.

"Hey, you guys want to do something?" I said.

Ariana remained still. "We are doing something."

"I mean besides tanning." I started drawing in the sand. With each furrow made, granules tumbled back in, half filling the indentation. Laying there doing nothing was not much different than sitting in school doing nothing. "And we've already got a tan."

"I want a *deep* tan."

Elle sat up as well. "Wanna get something to eat?"

Not really, I thought, but it was better than doing nothing.

"You two go without me," Ariana said, "so I can tan in peace."

Elle and I looked at one another and shrugged. Rising, we headed toward the white clapboard concession stand at mid-beach. Warm sand squished between my toes.

I ordered a lychee Hawaiian shaved ice, and Elle got sour gummies, her go-to whenever she was bored. We sat at a high top overlooking the beach.

"What's lychee taste like?" Elle said.

45

"Kind of like strawberry and pear mixed together," I said and held out my plastic teaspoon with a heaping of the white ice.

Elle leaned her mouth to the spoon, took it in, then grimaced. "Not my thing," she said then proffered the open bag of gummies to me.

I shook my head.

Brandon and his buddy had disappeared since the frisbee encounter, and as we ate I scanned for them on the horizon. Oh well, there were other fish. Maybe none as big as Brandon, but I'm sure they'd be tasty nonetheless.

"Looking for the frisbee boys?" Elle said.

"No. Yeah."

"I've heard the same thing that Ariana said about the guy talking to you. Story is it's a new girl every week. Don't be another notch in his belt."

"You're right, best to stay away from him."

She nodded.

I soon finished my shaved ice, but Elle was intent on getting through her entire bag of gummies before we left. The morning dragged on, as I rested my chin in hand, elbow propped on the table, the chair's flat, wooden seat pressing into my butt.

The first day of summer was turning out to be as magical as coleslaw.

***

"Hi Taylor."

My spirits went from 0 to 60 in an instant. I turned around on the high top. "Find your frisbee, Brandon?"

46

He gave a cocky half-smile. "Yeah. But lost Randy somehow."

"That's what you get for letting your stuff lie around. He'll show up."

"Hopefully not. Wanna go swimming?"

"Sure."

He reached out his hand, and I took it. I suddenly felt tingly all over.

I looked back over my shoulder at Elle, who shook her head.

We waded into cold Traverse Bay then once his body adjusted to the temperature he dove under. I glanced around for him, felt something grab my legs.

Squealing, I jumped, then Randy's hands grabbed my legs again from a different angle.

All right, two can play this game, I told myself, and dove in. His feet and that perfect ass of his faced me, as he circled back to where I'd been standing. A hurried two strokes later, and I pinched his toes.

He jumped up to stand, and I followed him, laughing. Sunlight glinted off his ice blue eyes, and wetness matted down his shaggy blond hair. He gave me his cocky smile again then brought his hands up and splashed water at me. I swung away and brought my arm up to block it, then swished water at him.

This is what summer is supposed to be, I told myself. Maybe Ariana and Elle were wrong about him. Even if he really was a player, I could enjoy his effort to seduce me, then wiggle away when he started to reel me in. I didn't have to sleep with him to have a good time.

We paused for a moment, catching our breaths. Elle's waving arms caught my attention.

She held both hands to the sides of her mouth. "I'm done with my gummies! Come back and tan with us!"

I looked back and forth between Elle and Brandon.

He locked onto my eyes and pointed. "See the island out there?"

"Yeah."

"Wanna check it out?"

To hell with tanning. "Okay."

***

"Know how to row?" Brandon said, as pulling the park service's rental to the water's edge.

"Is it just like a rowing machine?"

He nodded. "You take the back, and I'll push us in."

As I stepped over the boat's side, he tossed my bag and his small backpack in the boat's rear. No sooner had I taken a seat then he pushed the boat into the water, ran alongside it, and jumped in. Taking the front set of oars, he guided us on a course toward the clump of trees ahead.

I pulled the oars to my chest then pushed them away, as we made our way across the bay. My lungs were pumping, as the bay's waves pushed against us, but it wasn't anything we couldn't handle. The breeze on the water wicked off my sweat from the sun beating down on us and the exertion.

As Brandon rowed, I admired his thick arm muscles and sturdy back. Eye candy indeed. Truth was, he was doing most of the work but didn't seem to mind. He seemed too nice of a guy to be a player.

Within a few minutes, the evergreen island loomed before us. We rowed around to the back of it where there was a small lagoon. Our boat jolted as it hit sand, and he jumped out, grabbed the front rope, and lugged it and me ashore.

I stepped out, discretely rubbing my butt, sore from the rowboat's hard plastic. "Wow, you're strong."

He gave that cocky half-smile again and waved me off. "And I love the way your green eyes sparkle in the sun."

***

We walked hand-in-hand along a dirt path that circled the pine-studded island. The warmth of his touch washed away all of my worries.

"Been to the island before?" he said.

I shook my head. Ever since middle school, I'd wanted to go to the island, but none of my friends were up for it.

"It's got a cool sandstone cave. Wanna see?"

"Sure."

A few minutes later, we took a side path that headed down a small cliff to a narrow beach. A round black hole loomed in the sandstone wall.

We stepped in, the sound of the crashing waves behind us. Out of the sun, the temperature instantly cooled, and the light dimmed. My eyes adjusted, and I made out curved and polished boulders. Walking around one, the cave opened up with a high, circular ceiling.

"Very cool," I said.

He nodded and squeezed my hand.

I leaned against his hard body, and he wrapped an arm about my shoulders. For the first time, I caught his scent, sweet with hints of citrus.

I savored the cave's cold air prickling one side of my body and the warmth of Brandon's body on the other side. "What else is there?" I said.

***

When we finished the loop around the small island, Brandon grabbed his backpack from the rowboat and plopped down in the sand. I sat next to him.

"I worked up an appetite," he said. "Hungry?"

"A little."

He pulled out a big beach towel for us to sit on then red Gatorade and a package of color-matching licorice twists.

"Red is your favorite color?" I said.

"Green is now."

I grinned. "Blue is mine."

He handed me the bottle, and I took a swig.

"Smart boy," I said, "bringing candy that doesn't melt."

"Has your heart ever melted?"

"It might be melting now."

Damn it. I shouldn't have said that. His question – that was the line of a player.

But he didn't make a move. Instead, we chewed on our licorice sticks as sitting side by side, staring out at the lagoon. The water remained calm to the point of boredom and the horizon's frozen stillness spread out before us. There didn't seem to be a soul around; we had the island entirely to ourselves, and any bodies on the beach across the bay looked smaller than ants.

I twisted a strand of hair around my finger. Sitting was getting about exciting as a price war between two dentists.

So what if he was a player?

"Let's do something fun and wild," I said.

Brandon thought for a moment then got that sly smile again. "Have you ever gone skinny dipping?"

***

In the sun, my pubic hair shined like a jewel, as I tentatively stepped into the water. Wearing only my red bikini when Brandon suggested skinny dipping, I was practically naked anyway, so I was like *Hey why not?!*

We undressed at the same time, but Brandon hung behind as I got in the water, no doubt wanting to see my rear end. It looked better squeezed together by a bikini bottom, I thought, but I suppose a guy would be happy to see any young woman's bare butt.

Once in the water, Brandon and I swam, circling one another. He stopped and swept his hands across the surface, splashing water into my face. I squealed and dove under, grabbed at his cock like I was a snapping turtle. Jumping back, he slipped and went under. Rising, my breasts above the water line and dripping, I looked for him to make sure he was all right.

He shot up in the water right in front of me, and we laughed. Our eyes met, then he gently placed his hands on both sides of my shoulders. Slowly, our faces moved toward one another, then paused, and I caught a whiff again of his sweet and citrus scent. A moment later, our lips met.

I moaned into his mouth, as my hands tangled in his hair.

***

When I waded out of the water, my wet feet turned the beach sand to a soft mud that squished between my toes. The sun shined upon the lagoon in a warm, soft light.

As he emerged from the water, my eyes focused on his erection. It looked thick and stood tall, reaching his belly button. I bit my lower lip, wanted to trace the veins on his cock, to feel the soft skin over the hard rod.

"Just stand there," he said, "I want to look at you."

He slowly walked around me, taking me in, like I was an expensive sports car he'd always wanted. When he reached my backside, he leaned forward, and his tongue licked the edges of my ear, as an arm snaked around my waist, his large hand resting on my flat tummy.

My breath hitched, as his lips grazed my neck, skittering over the skin from below the ear to the collar bone. Goosebumps prickled. I arched my back against him, murmuring softly.

He pulled me back by the hair and locked his lips and teeth into my neck, sucking hard, then kissed and licked up to my ear, his large hand on my tummy holding me steady despite my weakening knees. My whole body pressed against him, and my bare ass found his hard cock. He rubbed it against the seam between my cheeks.

As Brandon rolled my ear lobe between his lips, I moaned, then his mouth went back down, gently biting my warm, wet neck. His hand on my tummy slid down to my pussy and rubbed its flush red folds, wet more from my juices than the bay water.

"You want to do something really wild?" he said.

"What's that?"

"Trust me." He let go and pointed to the big beach towel. "Lay down on your tummy."

I did.

"Good, now spread your legs."

My thighs scissored out, as he kneeled between them, my soaked, open pussy on full display for him.

His hand returned to my folds, and a finger found my clit. I gasped in pleasure, as he circled it, and my hands grabbed at the sand beside the towel. Another finger slipped into my hole, rubbed it from side to side.

Soft moans escaped my lips, as I found my head growing dizzy. My hips ground against him.

His finger in my hole slipped out, and slick with my juices, caressed the area around my netherhole. My eyes flew open, surprised not so much because of where he was touching me but at how pleasurable it felt, like his finger were caressing my areola. I didn't know that part of my body was so sensitive.

And then I gasped, as he slid the tip of his finger into my ass and rolled it back and forth.

"Ohh," I moaned.

He slowly spun his finger around in my ass then slid

it up and down, slowly going deeper. At first, my muscles resisted the pressure, but then the discomfort gave way as pleasure coursed through me like electric pulses. Somehow, through my ass, he was stimulating my hidden clitoris just beneath the skin of my nether tunnel.

I suddenly felt deliciously dirty, and my hips gyrated. This only helped his finger go deeper, stimulating more of my hidden clit. The towel beneath my pussy grew wet, as every muscle in my body tightened.

Then my body clenched and spasmed, leaving me shuddering and unable to control any part of my being. As my mouth opened in joy, I seemed to float. He'd given me my first anal orgasm.

The sun's warmth and gentle caress of his hand bathed me, as the hardness of his cock pressed against my thigh. My breathing and heart gradually slowed. I slowly rolled over, and he positioned himself between my legs, ready to take me.

But my palm rose to his chest. "Now you lay down," I said.

***

His eyes widened and mouth parted. After a moment, he moved to my side and reclined on the towel. I climbed into his lap, pressing my knees into his hips. Leaning down, our lips met and then opened. His tongue tasted sweet. I sat back up and reached my hand around to his cock, positioned it at my entrance.

"Take what you need," he said.

Oh, I intend to.

With his cockhead inside me, my palms pressed into the sand at our sides. I steadily lowered myself over his arousal, moaning the entire length. Once Brandon was completely sheathed inside me, I paused, luxuriated in the feeling.

I gave him a slow ride, as my thighs brought me up and down on his cock, my hips purling. He closed those beautiful blue eyes of his, and despite our act, looked so angelic, then he sighed in pleasure, his breathing deepening, and I smiled mischievously. I didn't love him, he didn't love me. We were just two people looking for relief from the boredom of life.

Leaning toward him, we kissed once more, and I rocked forward, as our breaths mingled. He grabbed my hips, meeting my unhurried rhythm with his own, as my hard nipples slipped along his chest. His cockhead bulged inside me; he was close.

His hands tightened their grip on my hips, as he made one last thrust then froze and groaned in pleasure. As his cum spurt inside me, my body shook, and I cried out.

***

Once my panting ebbed, I slid off Brandon and nestled next to him with my head on his chest.

My head still felt as if it was floating on air, and I began to imagine a summer of love together. No, I told myself, enjoy this moment – of us naked, our juices on one another, just the two of us lying in the sun like pagans.

After a while, he said, "We need to get the rowboat back."

"Yeah."

We washed ourselves off in the lagoon then after dressing boarded the boat and sluggishly rowed it toward the main beach.

"Wanna do something tonight?" I said.

He didn't answer for a moment, then "My parents have got something going on that I have to be at."

No, I don't regret it, I told myself as dipping the oars into the water. I got to have decent sex. I got to discover something about myself that I never knew before.

But those moments were all behind me. As the setting sun cast an orange glow across the bay, crossing the water back to Ariana and Elle seemed to take forever. I stared ahead at the distant shoreline, which looked like links in a chain.

Role Play

The goddamn phone rings, and I curse myself for bringing it to the pool with me. I ignore it, keep my eyes closed as lying in the lounge chair, soaking up the rays, pretending I'm in Maui. At last it stops, and I sigh in peace.

A beat later, it rings again. *Ugh.*

Lifting my sunglasses, I check the number. *Work.* Of course, *work.* I get one lousy week off a year, and they can't go a day without calling me. The place won't fall apart if I'm gone, for chrissakes...which, given all the hours I put in, actually is a depressing thought.

"Hello?" I say in as cheerful of a tone as I can muster.

"Guess what?" It's Aileen, my best friend since elementary school and now my coworker, two cubicles down.

"Grayer Corp. burned down, and we're out of a job?"

"I wish. But I do have good news, Marti."

"So good you couldn't wait to leave work to tell me? Cripes, I thought they wanted me to come in for something."

"Why, you with someone?"

"No."

"That explains why you're cranky."

"I don't need another boyfriend. Ever."

"Just because Ramon was an ass doesn't mean you should give up on men."

"You're a masochist, aren't you?"

"No, but I'm willing to try it." We giggle.

"So what's the good news?"

"Johnathan's plane arrives this afternoon."

"You called me because your geeky brother is coming home from the navy?"

"No, I called because we're throwing a welcome home party for him, and you're invited."

"Well–" I don't particularly feel like driving across Los Angeles during the evening commute.

"C'mon, what else are you doing besides hanging out at your apartment's crappy pool?"

"At least my apartment complex has one." Actually, I have a nice evening of lounging in sweats on my sofa with a bowl of popcorn and Netflix all planned out. "All right, where and what time?"

"That's the Marti I know." She gives me the details.

When she hangs up, I glance at the time on my phone. There are at least two good hours of not caring about a damn thing in the world left to me before I have to get ready. I close my eyes.

***

Cars pack both sides of the street in front of Aileen's childhood home. I have to park about four blocks away but tell myself not to get bitchy, if only for the sake of Aileen's parents, who I'm sure find this a joyous occasion. As for Johnathan's sake, I wear a baggy blouse. The little perv always was staring at my breasts

58

whenever I visited.

A big WELCOME HOME sign hangs over the garage, and I hear the crowd in the backyard on the patio. I follow the scent of grilled hamburgers to them.

"Marti!" Aileen shouts when she sees me turn the corner to the party. She marches on over, and we hug.

"This is quite the shindig," I say. "There's more people here than I expected." *Way more.*

"Johnathan is a popular guy."

"Sorry, am I at the right party? Do you mean Johnathan, as in your older brother?"

She giggles. "You're at the right place."

"So Aileen says you're going by 'Marti' now," a deep bass voice says.

I turn around. My mouth opens, but I don't say anything. Johnathan sports broad shoulders and a robust athletic build, like a football player. The navy did wonders for him. And his blue eyes – a woman could drown in them. When did those suddenly become attractive?

Finally I say, "Hello Johnathan."

"For a moment there, I thought you forgot my name."

And he *isn't* staring at my breasts.

"Martha sounded so...unprofessional," I say. His dirty blond hair actually works as a crewcut.

"'Marti' suits you. More grown up. How do you like working at Grayer?"

How do I like it? Too many people constantly gossiping and interrupting you with stupid questions. Too many tasks given to you at the last minute yet you're

59

responsible if it all goes awry. Too many middle-aged male coworkers hitting on me. "It's fine."

Aileen's mother sweeps in. "Marti! So glad you came!" Johnathan grins at his mother's unintended connotation; he's still a perv.

"Hi Mrs. Conlin," I say. "Thank you for inviting me."

"It's Torrie," she says. "Now that you're grown up, you call me by my first name."

Johnathan laughs. "Gee, everyone changed their names while I was gone."

Torrie presses her hand against Johnathan's shoulder, nudges him away. "Go say hi to the other guests. They're all here to see you."

"Yes ma'am," he says sheepishly and shuffles off.

"He's so much more...*compliant* since joining the navy," Torrie says. "Marti – Aileen and I have someone we'd like you to meet."

My eyebrows rise. So that's what this is really about.

She places her hand on my shoulder blade while Aileen takes my arm, and the two guide me toward their redbud tree. A skinny guy with horn-rimmed glasses leans all alone against it.

"Marti," Torrie says, "this is Garland. Garland, this is Marti."

He gives me a camera face smile. "Hello. Nice to meet you."

"Likewise."

We stand there awkwardly for a moment until Torrie speaks up. "Garland works with me at Slate's. He's an assistant project manager."

"Sounds interesting," I say, just a hint of sarcasm in my voice.

He doesn't pick up on it. "It is. We're working on next generation software that builds workflows and manages resources for business clients. The challenge is to synchronize the inputted data so it's useful for planning, forecasting, cost analysis, resource allocation, task management, and reporting."

"Wow, very impressive." The sarcasm is a little thicker.

"Well, it sounds like you two have a lot to talk about," Torrie says, as she and Aileen slink away.

Thanks a lot, Aileen. I glance over at her, and on the patio I see Johnathan staring at Garland, eyes narrowed and jaw clenched.

"If this software proves successful," Garland says, "I should get promoted to project manager."

I look away from Johnathan. "Oh. How long will that be?" Then I glance back at him. He's still stabbing Garland with dagger eyes.

"Probably two years. First we have to complete the project then let the Sales Department do its magic. What do you do for work? Any promotions coming up?"

"I work at Grayer with Aileen. Um, Garland, it's been nice talking to you. I need to take care of something now though."

"Oh, well maybe–"

I march right up to my best friend, as Garland's voice fades behind me. "What the hell was that, Aileen?" I say.

My best friend's jaw goes slack. "Mom and I thought

you'd two would make a cute couple."

I roll my eyes. "You ambushed me."

"What, you didn't like him? He's the take-charge type. Given how you always cheerfully accept those last-minute projects at work from Craig, I thought you were into that kind of guy."

"I take those assignments because I like to sleep with a roof over my head."

"Oh. I thought maybe it was because you liked Craig. Well, not Craig specifically but guys like him."

My hands roll into fists. "I can't think of a single woman in the world who likes guys like that."

"You mean you don't know any women who do. C'mon, you don't find the take-charge type sexy?"

OK, she has me there. So I harrumph. "I thought we were here to welcome Johnathan home."

With that, I turn to where Johnathan is on the patio, intent on starting a conversation with him, just to show Garland I'm definitely not interested.

I stop before taking a full step.

A blonde with long hair and blue dress clinging to every one of her curves is on Torrie's arm, laughing at something Jonathan said. His eyes focus on her. She touches his arm.

Slut.

That's not fair, I tell myself, *I would do the same thing if I liked a guy.*

I look at Aileen. "Seems like your mother is quite the matchmaker tonight."

Then I storm off, rounding the corner toward the

front of the house. Aileen calls after me, but I keep walking.

***

Day Two of vacation, and Aileen won't stop calling and texting me. I ignore all of it. Eventually I turn off the phone. I plan to call her back and apologize, but just not right now, not like I am *on demand*. I stretch out on the lounge chair, let the sun's warmth bathe me and embrace the stillness, the calm of it. By the time I get back to work, people will think I spent the week on a tropical beach getaway.

"Marti?"

The same deep bass voice I'd heard at the party. *Johnathan.*

I open my eyes. Dressed in khaki shorts and a black tee that hugs his thick arms, he stares down at my body, clad only in a skimpy bikini, breasts half hanging out. "Johnathan?"

And then she steps out from behind him. The blonde in the blue dress. Except today she wears a flowery sundress that perfectly matches the lipstick on her pouty lips.

"Aileen has been trying to reach you all day. She wants to apologize. She said you not responding is very unlike you. So I came over to make sure everything was okay."

Yeah, everything is okay. Almost. "I planned to call her back. Just needed some time to stew."

"I understand." An awkward moment of he staring at my almost nude body and me at his muscled arms

63

passes. "Um, this is Leeza."

Leeza sidles closer to Johnathan, takes his hand. "Hi."

I nod.

"We met at the party last night," he says.

I know. "Oh, how nice."

"So, everything is all right? *You're* all right?"

No, nothing is right. Not anymore. "I'm okay."

"I hope you'll call Aileen. She really does want to apologize."

Not simply "Call Aileen," given like an order? How refreshing. "Don't worry, I will."

"Great. Well, we'll let you be."

Leeza smiles at Johnathan like she can't wait to give him a blow job.

"Okay. Thanks for checking on me."

"Anytime."

They walk away, hand in hand, leaving me alone by the poolside. Funny how when you finally get what you want, you don't really want it at all.

***

The water fills my mouth, and somehow I am able to get my eyes above the surface and wave for help. Johnathan pulls his shirt over his head, revealing perfect six-pack abs, and dives into the pool. My head goes under, and I fight to hold my breath. An instant later, Johnathan swoops under me, and holding my shoulders above the water, swims to the pool's edge. He lifts me up, sets me at the lip, as he catches his breath.

"You scared me," he says.

With the air returning to my lungs, I gaze down at his

short-cropped hair and those broad shoulders.

He looks up, sees the lust in my eyes. It instantly fills his. His thumbs hook into the waistband of my bikini bottoms and pulls them down my legs and off. Then his large hands press against my inner thighs, pushing my legs apart, exposing me fully to him. Without hesitation, his tongue finds my clit, and my neck arches back, as I close my eyes and moan in pleasure.

And then those strong hands of his grip my waist and lower me back into the pool so that my open legs are level with his fully erect cock. He enters me, crushes me back against the pool's hard wall, as I wrapped my legs and arms around him for balance. I've never felt so full in my life.

His tongue slides across my breasts then flicks a nipple, as he slowly thrusts in and out. His eyes meet mine.

"I love you, Leeza."

My eyes fly open, as I awake. The orange sun sits just above the housetops, and I hope the sunscreen held out through the afternoon. My nose feels a little burned, but as I gaze down to the toes, my tummy and legs appear a golden tan. And then my face flushes red. A wet patch has formed on my bikini bottoms, right between my legs. I glance around, don't see anyone, thank God. *That was some dream, I guess.*

Standing, I tie the towel around my waist, head back to the apartment. *Time to call Aileen.*

***

"I really thought Gaylord and you would work out,"

Aileen says the next day, as we meet for dinner. "I'm sorry."

Quit apologizing. "I'm sure he's a nice guy. But he was way into his job more than anything else."

"Sounds perfect actually – that means you'd have a lot of time to yourself, which you seem to like. Anyway, I'm sorry again."

If you want to apologize for something, apologize for your mother introducing Johnathan to Leeza. Speaking of which... "How's this thing with Johnathan and what's her name working out?"

Aileen's brow furrows. "I'm not sure. At first, it seemed kind of magical how they got along so well. But she's the type who wants to play puppy dog to her master, and that's not Johnathan."

"You mean she likes to be on a leash in the bedroom?"

Aileen laughs. "No, I mean–"

"I know what you mean." A moment passes, as I take a long gulp of my beer. "So you don't think it'll last?"

"Not sure. He's matured while away at the navy. He used to do whatever he wanted, say whatever he thought."

"He used to put his foot in his mouth."

"That too. But now he's all courteous and helpful."

"We should send the navy a thank you letter."

"That's not a bad idea." She drank from her beer. "So is this all about Ramon?"

"Ramon? What do you mean?"

"Maybe you're not over him."

"And that explains why I wasn't into Garland, assistant project manager of boredom?"

"Yeah."

"Trust me, I stopped being into Ramon after I found out he'd fucked that blonde with the long hair." She looked a lot like Leeza, come to think of it.

"Okay."

"So if this Garland is so great, why don't *you* date him?"

"That would be awkward for my mom if we broke up."

I nod. "Come to think of it, it is about Ramon a little. Not directly though. I'm just tired of giving my all and getting nothing in return."

"Not all guys are like that."

"Which planet are you from again?"

"I'm just saying you should get out there. You deserve to be loved."

What I deserve is an orgasm that isn't courtesy of my Magic Wand. "Thanks, I appreciate that."

"I'm sure the right guy will come along soon."

I shrug. Maybe he already has.

***

Day Four of vacation, I head back to the bar and grille for dinner. Sitting by the pool every day has left me bored, and I'm starting to wonder if Aileen is right, that I should get myself out there again. I figure the best way to prove her wrong is to show up at this establishment, where there won't be a single decent man worthy of a relationship, let alone a one-night stand.

Stepping from the bright outside to the dark interior, my eyes take a moment to adjust. Then, as I head to a booth, there he is – Jonathan...and, of course, Leeza.

They sit across from one another, each leaning forward, smiling and conversing, their hands dangerously close.

And then the situation gets worse.

Garland steps in front of the booth. "Hi Marti," he says, a glass of something amber in his hand. "You ran off so quickly from the party."

"Oh hi, Garland," I say, as he slides into the seat across from me. *Aren't you first supposed to be invited to sit?*

"No need to explain, I understand. I'm glad we have another chance to get acquainted."

I let go a nervous giggle. *Swell.* "Oh, yeah, I...um...only just stopped in for a moment and have to..." *Have to do what? C'mon, think!*

And then I see Jonathan stealing glances at me. Wait, did he just throw an eye dart again at Garland?

"Actually, I don't need to get there right away, now that I think about it," I say. "How's the synchronization software coming along?"

"The next generation software that builds workflows and manage resources for business clients?" Garland says. "Quite well. The real challenge is to allow for flexibility and scalability, which is fraught with potential issues–"

I could care less, but I glance at Jonathan out of the corner of my eye. He's practically staring at Garland, who's oblivious to it. I smile at Garland, pretending to give him my full attention. He's happy to babble on.

A moment later, Jonathan abruptly rises, Leeza behind him. He glares at Garland one last time, and then they're out the door.

"In addition," Garland continues, "integration complexities pose a real challenge–"

I quick rise myself. "Actually, Garland, I just remembered, I need to be at the appointment at 5:30 rather than 6:30, so I need to run."

"Um, okay – maybe we could get together Fri–"

But I'm already halfway across the bar and grille, passing a waitress who gives me a confused look. A moment later, I'm back into L.A.'s blinding summer light.

***

Day Five of vacation, I head to a different bar and grille for dinner. I don't want to run into Garland again, so I might as well find a place I actually can eat this time.

Stepping inside, I scan for a place to sit then do a double take. Jonathan is at the bar. Alone. I wonder where the hell Leeza is. No extra drink on the bar, must not be here. Maybe he's waiting for her.

Only one way to find out.

"Hey Johnathan," I say, as taking the empty stool next to him.

He looks at me, and for a moment his blue eyes brighten. "Marti! What brings you here?"

"Hunger. And you?"

"Thirst." He tips his beer bottle toward me. Damn, his arm must be as thick as my neck.

"Where's Leesa?"

The color in his eyes dim at that. "It didn't work out."

Oh, that's too bad. "I'm sorry to hear that. Looked like you two were having fun."

He shrugs, and I swear I can see his muscles ripple under his button shirt.

"Well that explains your need for a beer. Want to get food with me?"

"Only if you get me another beer to go with it."

"Deal. So why didn't it work out?"

"She's not my type."

"What type is that?"

He gazes a long moment at me. "I've never felt comfortable being the one in charge where women are concerned. But that's what she was looking for. And when I didn't behave the way she wanted, she let me know what a disappointment to maledom I was."

"Hmm. I'm sure the right girl will come along soon."

"You sound like my sister."

I nudge him to look at an empty booth in the corner. "Let's talk about it over a plate of loaded nachos."

He nods and follows me to the booth, our sandals squeaking on the sticky floor. A waitress quickly takes our order.

Once we're alone again, I continue. "So is that why you joined the navy? To feel more...manly with women?"

"I was just a skinny kid who never listened to

anybody because I didn't want to get caught up in their games, ya know? Thought if I talked a good show they'd think I was more than what I really was and leave me alone."

"Makes sense."

"What about you? Last I heard, Aileen said you were going out with some guy, a Raymond?"

"Ramon. And that's long over. Cheated on me. So you asked about me while away?"

His face flushed red. "Sure. Didn't you know I had a crush on you when we were teenagers?"

"When we were teenagers, you always were staring at my breasts."

"What can I say? I was a teenage boy, and they were gorgeous."

"You could have been less obvious about it."

He looks down at the table. "I'm sorry. I didn't mean to make you feel uncomfortable."

Our nachos and two beers arrive. We dig in, and I'm hungrier than I thought. Suntanning is hard work, I guess.

After a few bites, I say, "Why didn't you ask me out?"

"Ask out my baby sister's best friend? That would have been awkward."

"It would have been awkward if *I* was the older one."

He shrugs. "Guess I lacked the confidence."

And you still apparently do, at least by Leeza's reckoning. "Look, Johnathan, you've got nothing to be afraid of where women are concerned. You're a good looking man in great shape. The navy turned you into a courteous gentleman. Any woman would want that. You saw how Leeza fawned all over you."

"You make it sound easy. Like anything, it's a learned skill and one that I have little practice at."

"What, no woman waiting for you in every port of call?"

He grinned, shook his head.

"Look, when we're all done here, let's walk back to my place, and we'll role play through it."

"Role play?"

"I'll pretend to be a man, and you'll pretend to be a woman I'm hitting on."

He laughed. "With your breasts, you never could pull off being a man."

My turn to laugh. "Perv."

For a long moment he says nothing. "Okay, I'll try it. What have I got to lose?"

Just your dignity? "Nothing at all."

***

I've never really coveted the traditional male role of being in charge. I've really never wanted to be the subservient female either, though at work that's what I've ended up being. A little pendulum swing to being a man, even if only in play, might actually do me good, help recenter me.

We sit next to each other on my beat-up sofa. "All right, let's pretend we're at a party. I'm the guy who spots this hot girl on the sofa. So I sit down next to her. Listen to how I flirt."

He nods.

I put on my best smile. "Hey, how it's going? I'm Johnathan."

"Hi. I'm...Marti."

"I noticed your Chainsmokers shirt. That's my favorite band!"

He looked down at his plain denim blue shirt that he filled out so nicely. "Yeah, I love all of their songs."

"Which is your favorite?"

"*Roses*, by far."

"Wait, are you a Chainsmokers fan?"

His nose and forehead scrunch up. "Yeah, I'm wearing a T-shirt with them on it."

"No, I mean are you, Johnathan, a Chainsmokers fan?"

He shrugged. "Yeah."

"That's awesome! OK, see what I did there?"

"Yeah, you broke character."

"No dummy, I started by introducing myself. If you give your name, she'll probably give you hers. Then I tried to find a connection so we had something to talk about."

"So if you have a script when you go in, that makes it easier?"

Boy, he really doesn't know what he's doing. "Yes. It helps you with your confidence because your mind won't go blank when you try to talk."

He nods. "Okay, then what?"

"If the conversation keeps going, take it up a notch. Start complimenting her."

His face looks blank.

"All right, pretend I'm the man again. Your hair is

beautiful, it really brings out the color in your eyes."

He runs his hand in a wavy motion as if touching his hair and in a falsetto voice says, "I only wash it with salt water."

I laugh, punch him in the arm. "Shut up you goofball. See, you've got it down already. You're flirting with me."

"So how do I know that a girl is interested while we're flirting?"

"Well, she'll give off all kinds of body signals. She might lock her eyes onto yours." I find his gaze and kept it. "She might brush her hair behind her ear, exposing her neck." I demonstrate the move. "She might sidle up closer." I scoot my butt across the cushion so our arms and thighs touch.

"And how do you know when to go in for a kiss?"

"How about right now?" My mouth moves to his, and our lips brush against one another. His touch is feather-light and ever so slowly increases in pressure. My body goes dizzy, as if it's stepped outside into a heat wave.

I began to back off, but he wraps a hand around the nape of my neck and pulls me in one more time. His tongue slides over my mouth until I eagerly open for him. Our tongues entwine, shallow and light and first, then faster and deeper. When we both withdraw from one another to catch some air, my heart is hammering

"Like that?" he says.

"Yeah, just like that," I say, still breathy.

His large hand caresses my cheek, and he slowly leans toward me. An electric pleasure flows through me, as his lips press against the nape of my exposed neck.

His warm breath washes across my throat, as he kisses upward toward my ear, and I swoon. Then he works his way back down my neck along my shoulder, pulling aside the collar of my blouse to access my bare skin.

"Wait a moment," I say.

After a moment of nuzzling, he reluctantly pulls back. I tug the blouse over my head and toss it onto the floor. Then my arms go behind my back, unclasp the bra, and it falls before me to the sofa.

"I know you've always wanted to see these."

His eyes widen, and he lets out a gasp of amazement. "They are beautiful."

I almost say, *Do they bring out the color in my eyes?* but before I can, his large hand, with the gentlest touch, circles my breast, slowly making its way toward the nipple. Before reaching it, he stops and does the same to my other breast. Waves of pleasure run through me. As his hand returns to the first one, he gently squeezes as working his way around the globe.

My panting increases, and my breasts grow fuller, as he does his magic upon them. Then, as he reaches my nipple, with a single finger he traces and slowly rubs it in different directions. I close my eyes and moan deeply. He repeats with the other breast.

The whole world seems to shrink. There is no one in it but Johnathan and me, and the center of that world are his hands upon my breasts.

He cups each of my globes and leans toward them. Gently breathing warm air directly onto a nipple, his tongue follows, as he licks in a circular motion around it.

My head tilts back, as if somehow I might get more air that way, and both of my nipples harden.

Two of his fingers slide around each bud, then when his fingertips arrive, he gently rolls them and pinches. Every muscle in my body tenses, as I gasp, and the wetness grows between my legs.

As he lets go, my pleasure recedes, then he slowly pinches again, this time adding a slight twist. Releasing my nipple, he pauses for a second, then pinches once more, this time tighter than the last and twists it even farther.

"Oooh fuck..." I say.

He pauses for a long moment then pinches and twists the other way with the most intensity yet. My muscles tighten even more, and when he pinches and twists once again, I shake uncontrollably, then scream and gasp in pleasure. I collapse forward into him, catching my breath, and he holds me, as gently stroking my back.

"Wow, that sort of snuck up on me and exploded out of nowhere," I said. "I've never had a nipple orgasm before."

"I see your breasts are extremely sensitive."

I nod as coming back down to earth. Determined not to let him get away like Leeza did, I find the energy to keep going and got down on the carpet before him. *Damn, this is tough, usually I do all of my work before cumming.* "Okay, let me show you just good I can make you feel." My fingertips run up the length of his thigh.

He grabs my wrist. "No."

I look up at him. "No?"

"If your breasts are so sensitive, I have something else that you might like."

***

I look up at him with uncertainty and anticipation.

"No matter what, I want you to maintain eye contact with me. Okay?"

He's got me wondering now. I nod.

We stare into one another's eyes, and his open palm slaps the side of a breast.

I let out a yelp, and yet...something felt electrifying about it.

His palm slaps the side of the other breast, as we keep our eyes locked, and I find my pussy growing wet again.

He slaps both breasts once more, then under each one, then down at an angle, then mixes it up, slapping a little harder each time. My breathing turns ragged, and my heart quickens; somehow the pain and humiliation of each slap shouldn't have me longing for his cock deep inside me. The staccato slaps echo off my apartment walls, and he lightens then increases the force of the strikes, as well as their rhythm and the unpredictability of giving control to Johnathan has me almost ready to give my entire self to him.

I feel my breasts swelling, the nipples hardening again, and he pauses, searching my eyes for the unmistakable sign that I'll submit. Then he gives a single hard slap to the side of one breast and then the other, and I squirm.

He caresses the back of my head then wraps the hair

around his palm and pulls. I shriek.

Holding my head in place, he slaps my breasts with the front of his palm then backhands them. I moan deeply, and if he ripped off my panties, he'd find I was more than wet enough to receive him.

He massages and squeezes a breast, then his warm, moist mouth offers relief until he pulls back and slaps it. I'm whimpering, half in pain, half in need.

His lips go to my other breast but focuses on the nipple, rolling it between his tongue, lightly biting it, barely running his teeth over it. The moment his mouth leaves, he slaps the breast, with the nipple at the center of his palm.

Johnathan lets go of my hair, and he cups one breast and slaps, fast and hard, over and over. My hips are gyrating, thrusting on an imaginary cock, and he takes hold of the other breast, repeats his punishment.

At last he stops and pulls back.

I wait for him to tell me what to do.

He stands. "Take off the rest of your clothes and get in the position that you want to be fucked."

***

Broken from the thrill of submitting, I'm now asked to be in charge again. A small smile tugs at the corner of my lips. *Time to add a new twist to this game.*

I kick off my sandals, turn at the waist to flash my attributes to him, then slide my hands down my front from the breasts to the pants. There, my fingers unbutton the jeans, and I shimmy them downward until gravity takes over.

His breathing grows heavier.

I turn around, shake my butt, then jut it out and roll my panties down my thighs until they fall to the jeans. Stepping out of them, I twirl toward him, giving him a good look at what he really wants to see.

He's fully hard.

Turning around, I wiggle my butt – there's more to me just my breasts after all – and cover both globes with my hands. Pirouetting to face him, I lean forward then remove my hands.

With that, I stand straight and stare at him.

"You want to be fucked standing up?"

Smart ass. "First take off your own damn clothes. And make it worth my time to watch."

His face pinkens at that. As kicking off his sandals, though, his expression turns serious, and he gradually gyrates his hips, doing a slow dirty dance. Johnathan's fingers go to his shirt buttons, undoes them one at a time, then his palm runs down his chest and tummy, and I wish that were my hand, but I merely stand and watch; forcing him to fulfill my instructions is part of my game. He shrugs the shirt off his wide shoulders, lets it slide down his arms and off him to the floor.

Jonathan's hips keep moving forward, like he's thrusting inside a woman, but I'm too enamored with his six-pack abs to think about that. Then he unbuttons his jeans, slowly brings the zipper down and turns around, gives me a good look at his pert butt as he teasingly brings both his pants and boxers down his cheeks and over his thighs. The jeans and boxers pass his knees then puddle at the floor.

My pussy tightens and grows wet.

I think he's been fooling me. He knows more about what he's doing then he lets on. Or maybe that was all part of the role play?

Johnathan slowly turns around, and there he is, my best friend's big brother, butt naked. His erect cock sticks straight out, as he continues to purl his hips back and forward. He stares at me.

Stepping up to him, I push his chest so that he falls back on the sofa. "Save a horse, ride a cowboy," I tell him.

I crawl onto his lap, bend my knees and press them against his hips. My pussy finds his cock, and I press down, engulfing it, letting go a long moan of pleasure as I do

After a couple of slow slides up and down on him, his large hand presses me midback, pushes me forward so our faces me. He wraps his arm around my back, holds me there as he thrusts in and out. His free hand goes to my butt and palms a bouncing ass cheek. I bite my lower lip, gasping for breath.

My breasts slide against his chest, and our sweat acts like a salve after his slapping. To my delight, as my globes pressed against him, his cock hardened even further.

His hands wrap around my ribs, brings me up so I'm sitting on him, then slides to my breasts. Pleasure spirals through me, as he squeezes them then plays with my nipples.

My palms press against his chest, and I gaze down at him. He gasps and moans, as I ride up and down his cock. His eyes are closed, and a look of utter ecstasy fills his face.

I smile at it and pick up speed.

My sweaty hair falls into my face, as my body increasingly tenses. His whole body grows rigid, and he's near too.

Then a long moan escapes both of our mouths, as I throw my head back and receive his cum.

For several long moments, my body feels as if it's engulfed in a warm heat swaying to the deep, gentle ripples of my second then third explosion.

***

Day Six of vacation begins with sunlight breaking through the edges of the bedroom blinds. My heads rests on Jonathan's broad chest, and his thick arms wrap around my slender back. A warm, peaceful glow envelops us.

My eyes look up at his face. "Say, I think you know a little more than you're letting on."

His face pinkens again. How had I never noticed this quirk in him when younger? "Yeah, I was just playing with you earlier," he says. "I've been in the navy for four years, ya know."

Of course he'd be experienced, how couldn't I have thought that? "Then why'd you lead me on?"

"Because I knew the only way to get you in my arms was to let you live a fantasy."

"Well, I like the reality of where I am right now."

He caresses my hair. "I'm glad."

I glance at my bedstand clock. There are at least 48 good hours of not caring about a damn thing in the world left to me before I have to get ready for work.

My hand reached for Jonathan's half-erect cock and slowly strokes it back to fullness.

Pearl Necklace

"Why is he even on this field trip?"

Six girls sat in the bus seats surrounding Tony, their bouncy laughs coming too quick and far too loud as they talked to him. He just sat there all cool in his sunglasses, flashing his boyish grin.

"Breanna Wilkes, you're not jealous are you?" my best friend Jody said from the seat next to me.

"I thought you were on my side."

"I am. But don't you think you're overreacting?"

My lip curled. "He spent time in juvie. He's not in college to learn – just to steal." *Steal and break everyone's hearts, by the looks of it.*

"Looks like he's stolen your common sense. We're on this trip to learn about art and have a little fun – don't ruin it by obsessing over him."

"I'm *not* obsessing."

She giggled at that. "Whatever."

Maybe she was right. I kept staring at him – his thick, dirty blond hair, his strong chin, and those slightly hooded blue eyes – and my own eyes grew narrower the longer I did.

Jody glanced over at me then back at Tony. "You're only upset because you can't have him."

"I could, *if* I wanted to."

"Not the way you hide your breasts."

"Whadya mean? With my breasts' size, there's no way to hide them."

"You know what I mean. I've never seen you shove them in a guy's face or wear anything lowcut."

"I'm *not* a slut."

"Your loss."

"How can you say that? You're not slutty."

"And I don't have breasts like yours either. Just chill. Look out the window for a while. The autumn leaves are really pretty right now."

I rolled my eyes, but Jody did get me to thinking. Was she saying she would be a slut if she had large breasts like me? That I should be loose because of my breast size? Why was I even thinking about these questions?

"I'm an artist," I said. "That's my focus right now."

Jody's turn to roll her eyes. "Right."

I crossed my arms and looked out the window, trying to ignore Tony, all of the Art Club girls hitting on him, and Jody. Mhm, she was right, the fall colors were quite striking.

***

At the art museum, Jody and I walked through a gallery of French illustrators from the early 1900s. Several were portraits of women, almost all showing them in some forlorn emotional state with just the slightest hint of sensuality.

"These look a lot like your paintings as of late," Jody said.

"Something about this style and subject matter

speaks to me. I wish I could paint as well as these artists."

"Breaking up with Delbert was a good thing for you, I think," Jody said. "You've been super-creative ever since."

"You mean 'I have a lot of emotions to process.' That's what my art is about right now. There's nothing 'super-creative' going on."

"You do have one quality of a great artist that really stands out."

"What's that?"

"You doubt yourself all of the time."

I stopped at a drawing of a woman lying on a bed, her softly draped clothes a textbook in light and shadow. The woman held the back of her hand to the forehead with eyes closed. I'd spent a few days lying in the same position on my bed after breaking up with Delbert.

I wondering why he no longer loved me. Probably because I'm a shy and quiet girl who prefers her paints and canvas to the nightclub, probably because when I did speak I was always bitching about something, a side effect of always have a sore back thanks to my large breasts. For some reason, he always wanted me to flatten my hair, as that was the style of the day, but I preferred my frizzy mane.

"Oh look who's over there," Jody said. "You're not going to have another meltdown, are you?"

I followed Jody's eyes to the far side of the gallery where Tony examined a framed illustration as the other Art Club girls flitted about him. "And why again is he on this trip?"

"Because he's interested in art."

"If you call 'graffiti' art."

Jody waved her hand dismissively. "If it bothers you so much, go ask him."

"We've got nothing to say to one another."

"You're just afraid."

"That sounds like a dare."

"It was. You've been afraid of talking to guys ever since breaking up with Delbert."

Had I been? I gazed at Tony, his thick hair and strong chin prominent in the gallery's lights, wondering why his art unfairly got all of the attention while I got none, especially when he didn't belong here at all. The time had come to finally put him in his place.

"All right, I'll show you," I said to Jody and then gulped as taking my first step toward him.

***

Tony gazed at the drawing, a portrait of a redheaded woman wearing a pearl necklace, a strap on her silky camisole hanging loosely on an arm.

"I like the artist's soft tonal variations," I said.

"Her style feels both sensual and somber, an interesting juxtaposition," he said.

Mhm, maybe he was smarter than I gave him credit for. "I'm Breanna," I said.

He nodded. "I know who you are. I'm Tony – but you probably know that already too."

"I do. A lot of people talk about you, Tony. Some say you were in juvie."

His gaze turned to the next illustration in the series, of a woman whose face peered through a partially opened door.

"And you don't like to talk about that?" I said.

"I really liked your two paintings in the student exhibit at the Fine Arts gallery, Breanna. They are reminiscent of this artist's style."

Uh, maybe he knew more about art than I thought. "Thanks." He *liked* my work. But he was still a thief. Maybe. "Want to get a coffee?"

He turned to me. For the first time up close, I saw his eyes, blue as a flame. "Sure."

We left the gallery, as the other Art Club girls looked incredulously at us, and re-entered the main hall, where a coffee bar sat across the way. After the barista served up our orders, he guided me to a table against the wall and behind all of the other seating.

"Don't want to be seen with me?" I said.

"I'm trying to avoid the other Art Club girls. They've been flocking around me the whole trip."

"I thought you liked that."

"It's flattering but gets tiring after a while. I'm interested in art. That's what I want to focus on."

"Yeah?"

"I've always liked to draw. It took me away from this world and all of the bad things in it."

"It's like you're creating your own world on the page or canvas."

He leaned forward. "Exactly. Someone who doesn't understand that would just be a distraction to me right now."

"Having someone in love with you *isn't* a distraction. It's a blessing."

"You think so? But just as what is art versus decoration, one might ask what is love versus infatuation? Have you ever been with anyone?"

He didn't sound at all like someone who'd been in juvie. "I've had a boyfriend."

"I didn't ask if you had a boyfriend. I asked if you had ever *been with* anyone?"

I blushed. Did he think I was asexual or something? "We did it once or twice."

"'Once or twice'? You don't remember?"

"Twice."

"What was he like?"

"He wanted to be an accountant. So he was very orderly and logical about everything while I was more the messy, creative type."

"I didn't mean what was his personality."

My brow furrowed. "Oh – you mean what was he like in..."

He nodded. "Yeah, in..."

My cheeks burned red. How did we get on the topic of sex? "Well...a bit boring if truth be told."

"Uncreative?"

"Yeah, it was like he was groping me then wham bam and it's all ov–" I stopped myself, couldn't believe what I'd just said.

"So Breanna wants a lover who takes his time."

I blushed again. Delbert never talked this way with

me. "Well, yeah, doesn't every woman?"

He shrugged. "Some do, some don't."

"And you speak from experience?"

That boyish grin crossed his face again. "Which painters influenced your art?"

"You never answered my question back in the gallery about being in juvie."

"My question first."

"I've been influenced by everything I've seen. I think what often happens to an artist is they have their own style or a vision of what they want to create and then discover it's similar to someone else's and so learn about that person and their works, and that becomes a great influence."

Tony nodded as considering what I said. "That certainly was the case for me. Now your question. Yeah, I was in juvie. I allegedly broke through a fence – but truth is there already was a hole in the fence, I just separated it a little more to slip through – and burglarized a place."

"Why did you rob a house?"

"Robbery is when you commit a crime against a person and take something. Burglary is just breaking in and taking something. I'm not a robber."

Uhn, who knew? "Why did you burglarize a house?"

"I was hungry. I needed money."

I wanted to ask a thousand more questions about that but decided it best not to.

***

Tony finished his coffee in a long gulp then stood up.

"I want to see the Monet and Picassos," he said. "Maybe we could catch up later."

I nodded, and he was off, leaving his empty cup across from me. Somehow, though, I couldn't get angry at him for it, like I did with Delbert, who never picked up after himself.

So I sat there sipping my coffee, wondering what Delbert was doing now. Probably in class learning about double-entry statements or some accounting crap like that. Probably enjoying it, too, in that twisted way some people really get off on moving meaningless, imaginary numbers around, not at all examining how light and color were expressed in *Japanese Bridge and Water Lilies* like Tony soon would be.

I couldn't believe the conversation we'd just had. Tony wasn't supposed to have eyes that blue or a smile that warm. And he wasn't supposed to talk to me.

I picked up his empty cup and tossed it with mine into the trash. I had a Renoir to see.

***

I took a seat next to Jody in the museum's auditorium, waiting for the lecture on how artists have reframed the female figure through the centuries.

"I see you two had coffee," she said. "Ooh la la."

"He might be more interesting than I thought."

Jody gave me a sly grin, as the emcee stepped before the crowd and welcomed us.

And then up near the front, right in my line of sight with the speaker, I saw him.

One of the girls from the bus sat next to Tony, her

shoulder pressed against his. Uninvited jealousy heated my chest. I looked back and forth between the two, couldn't concentrate on the lecture. Crossing my arms, I stared and stared and stared.

And then the speaker stretched his arms out. "These artists show us that the secret to success is to let go, to not hold back your creativity, or you'll never be more than one of the crowd."

Everyone clapped and rose to leave. *What, it's over already?*

"You can quit scowling now," Jody said. "She's no longer sitting next to him."

***

Jody and I rolled our suitcases into the hotel room. We had a whole morning of lectures to hear before leaving Philly the next afternoon for the long drive back to Mathewson.

Plopping on the bed nearest the window, Jody kicked off her shoes and rubbed her soles. "I think I saw more great art today than I've seen all the rest of my life."

I fell back on the bed and stared at the ceiling. "Tell me about it. Both Renoirs' and Cézanne's *The Bathers*."

"Van Gogh's *Sunflowers*."

"Toulouse-Lautrec's *Moulin Rouge, The Dance*. Avril's *Necklace and Camisole*."

"Avril? Who's that?"

"You know, that first exhibit we went to, of the French illustrators."

"You mean the one where you talked to Tony?'

"Yeah that one."

"No wonder you remember those drawings."

"Tony has nothing to do with it." I got up to wash my face and ready myself for bed.

"In a museum with Picasso, Chagall, and Monet, you remember...what's his name? Avril?"

"It has nothing to do with Tony," I said as digging through my toiletries bag. "Hey, did you bring any makeup wipes with you?"

"You know they're bad for your face."

"They're convenient."

"Leaves you more time to focus on your art. Right?"

"Right!"

"They've got a store that sells toiletries near the checkout desk."

"I'll be back in a second."

***

The hotel store had makeup wipes, and though they were overpriced I still bought them. As the clerk ran my credit card, I spotted Tony walking across the lobby toward the elevator, carrying something in a plastic bag. I watched him from the corner of my eye, but as soon as the clerk gave me back my card, I stuffed it in my pocket and double-timed it over to the elevator.

I squeezed in just before the door closed.

"Hey Breanna." He stood there, one thumb in his pocket as leaning against the elevator wall.

"Hi Tony."

He grinned. "In a rush?"

"Don't want me riding the elevator with you?" I held my hands behind my back.

"No problem with you being in the elevator," he said then held up his bag. "But I am carrying Man vs. Fries."

"It smells good."

"My point exactly."

"You can trust me. I'm a good girl."

"That's too bad."

The thought struck me that we were flirting. Was I really interested in a guy like Tony? I thought about Delbert a guy with a future, president of two clubs...and also straight-laced and predictable, someone who never let loose. *Yeah, who am I kidding? I never let loose...*

"Ever have Man vs. Fries?"

I shook my head.

"There's plenty here. Come join me."

I looked at the floor and shifted my foot as the elevator came to stop. "Okay."

Though he couldn't have been in his room for more than a few minutes during our trip, it already was a mess – he'd dumped out his duffel bag onto a bed, and the contents of his toiletries kit were scattered around the bathroom sink. He pulled the table out from the room's corner and positioned two chairs on either side of it. Then he unpacked the bag of food.

"NorCal Asada Fries," he said.

A Styrofoam container of French fries sat beneath drizzles of cheese, sour cream, guacamole, and some sauce, a work of art itself. "Looks delicious."

We each took a bite, and it was. For a while, neither of us said anything, just ate, licking our messy fingers after every bite.

"May I ask you a question?"

He shrugged as gazing at me and eating another cheese-covered fry.

"When you burglarized that house, why were you hungry?"

"My mom was a meth addict. She was out of it most nights."

"Most nights? Did you commit other crimes?"

"Yeah. Pickpocket wallets. Steal from unlocked cars and pawn the stuff. Whatever I needed to get by. But in juvie there was this correctional counselor who looked out for me after he saw I could draw. Once I got out, he took me in, made sure I stayed on the straight and narrow, and nourished my interest in art."

"And here you are."

"And here I am. And what about you, Breanna Wilkes? How did you get here?"

"Not quite as interesting as a story. Always like to draw and paint as a kid. Took a lot of high school art classes. Went to a college with a great program."

"Not that, Breanna. How did you get to be so good at painting?"

I blushed. Somebody finally recognized my talent, and it had be a guy like Tony. "I didn't exactly go on dates. So weekend nights were spent developing my skills."

"That's surprising."

"What's surprising?"

"That you didn't date. You're quite attractive. The way your hair waves about your face – it has a wildness to it."

I laughed. "I'm definitely not wild."

"Maybe you should let go."

"And where would that get me? I don't exactly have the body of a model."

Tony shrugged. "It's not the body so much as the attitude. Besides a little meat on the bones is much better than a skin and bones girl."

"What I'd give to be skin and bones. Then I wouldn't have to carry around these big breasts. Some days my back hurts like hell because of them."

"Most guys think big breasts are hot."

"Not mine apparently."

"Try being wild then." He stuffed a fry dripping in cheese and guacamole into his mouth.

He sounded like Jody, but I wasn't going to tell him that. "Yeah. Like how?"

He finished chewing and stuck his finger toward me. "Lick it off."

I chuckled, realized he was serious, and thought a moment about it. *Why not?*

So I leaned forward, ran my tongue across his finger, then leaned even closer and wrapped my lips around it. For a moment, I imagined it was his cock in my mouth. *Breanna Wilkes, behave yourself.*

I slowly slid my mouth off his finger, leaving it completely clean.

He nodded slightly as looking over his finger. "You said your back hurts. Come over to the bed, and I'll give you a massage."

***

Tony had me sit on the floor against the bed while he positioned himself atop the bed behind me, his legs framing my body. His hands draped over the top of my shoulders, and he gently squeezed up on the muscles.

My eyes closed. "Mmm, that feels good."

The tips of his fingers pressed into the muscles from the inside of the shoulders then outward. My blouse scrunched up wherever he rubbed. With each slow, smooth motion across my back, though, the tension evaporated from my head.

"Your hair is beautiful – it's a perfect match for your eyes," he said barely above a whisper.

After kneading for a few minutes, he changed direction and worked his way toward my back's center. I wanted to purr like a cat.

He tugged lightly at my blouse. "Take this off; it's keeping me from reaching every part of your back."

I leaned forward, pulled the blouse over my head. *Now he'll able to see my breasts through my bra*, I thought.

But Tony had other ideas. "Lean your head back."

I did. With the crown of my head almost touching his crotch, his fingers moved up and around my forehead in a circular motion. He went back and forth across it several times. His hands smelled like the asada I'd licked from his fingers. His fingers moved downward to the narrow space between my eyes and hairline. A warm, floaty feeling enveloped me.

Tony's fingers caressed their way along the sides of

my cheeks to my neck then back across my shoulders. Then his palms gently pressed me forward, and his hands kneaded my upper back, sending my mind into some kind of somnolent bliss.

"You're super-tense. These traps are like rocks."

His fingers reached my bra, and unclasping it, he pulled the straps down onto the arms. My breasts tumbled out as the bra fell into my lap.

His palms rested against my mid-back and slowly circled up to my shoulders. Then his fingers stretched out and with his thumb he made deeper spirals down the length of my back. His thumbs rubbed upward again and just above my ribs worked their way around to my front.

When he reached my breasts, the pads of his fingers lightly circled around and up them. My pulse raced. Reaching the top of them, he caressed the skin just above my nipples, and suddenly there was nothing in the world but his fingers and my breasts.

His hands withdrew from my body, and I almost moaned in disappointment, as my eyes slowly opened.

"Go lay on the bed so I can massage your lower back," he said.

I did – without putting back on my bra or blouse – and Tony sat alongside me. He reached one palm to my far hip while the other rested on the near hip. He slowly pulled one hand toward him as the other one pushed away. He repeated this as incrementally working up to mid-back and then back down again to my waist. I turned to putty.

After the third time of doing this, his fingers pushed down my jeans and panties a little, and he repeated the move again across the top of my ass then up to my mid-back and down once more. When he reached the edge of my jeans, his hand slipped under me, and unsnapped them. He slid them off and then the socks, too, so I lay there in only my panties.

His strong hands worked their way up my calves and thighs, and the closer he got to my pussy, the wetter I grew. At the top of my thigh, he caressed my tight ass cheeks, pushing the panties so they rested scrunched up in my crack. Then his hand slid between my legs, and I knew he could tell I was soaked down there.

He wasted no time pulling down my panties to past my knees then removing them altogether.

A lone finger circled my pussy's entrance, opening me, making me wetter with each orbit. I let out a low moan, and he slowly pressed just part of his finger inside me then slowly pulled it out, going deeper with each thrust. Quiet gasps escaped my mouth, and once he got in all the way, my pussy walls grabbed his finger. He kept it still until I let it go then he whirled his finger so that it spiraled in and out of my pussy like a screw going in and out of a board. I bit my lower lips as his twisty thrusts gained in speed. Delbert never was this good.

The heat in my pussy spread to my tummy, swirling and rising, building and building until before I knew it, it had taken over my whole body. My nipples hardened, and I grew wetter, as the pressure swelled and throbbed and tensed, and then in an instant came release as I screamed in satisfaction.

***

I rolled over on to my back as Tony took off his shirt. There on his chest was a tattoo of Picasso's *The Dream*, the one where a woman's head leans to the side, her breast half bared beneath a pearl necklace. I sat up, traced it with my fingers.

"A little secret only you know," he said.

I gazed into his eyes. "Tony, I... I don't want to have sex. I don't want to risk getting pregnant. I...I mean I appreciate that you helped me cum, but–"

He cupped my cheek. "I understand. I might have some other way that you could please me."

"Oh?"

I watched him finish undressing. His cock looked big in his boxers, but when he pulled them down, my throat caught. For a moment, my eyes trailed along his erect cock, it as hard as one of the museum's marble statues, it sticking straight up, the bulbous head nearly reaching his belly button. *Yum.*

"Lay back down, on your back," he said.

***

When I did, he straddled me at the waist, his knees on each side of my ribs, then shifted closer to my chest, his erect cock bobbing just inches before my chin. He spit into his hand then wiped the saliva around his cock. Taking it by the base, he guided it between my two breasts; the globes parted ways for his erection then rolled back, partly covering him.

"Hold your breasts together," he said.

I pushed them toward one another, held his cock snugly. Delbert never would have thought of doing this.

Tony slowly began to thrust. My breasts squished against his cock, as it slid back and forth, and my pussy turned sopping wet again. Finally I was grateful for big breasts; no little size one girlie like the others in the Art Club could please Tony this way.

His thrusts grew in speed, and his cock's mushroom head poked out between the top of my breasts. I propped my head up on a pillow and watched it. A couple of thrusts later, the cockhead was soaked in precum, and I looked up at Tony.

His eyes were closed and mouth open in pleasure, as his chest heaved, his cock sliding between my breasts. My hands gripped his hips that swayed toward and away from me.

Tony moaned loudly, as he threw his head back, and his cockhead broke through the top of my breasts. His cum fired in three spurts, first across a cheek, then directly in my eye, and the third from the bridge of my nose straight down to my lips.

He took a moment to come down from his dizzy high, and breathing hard, looked at me. His finger went to my closed eye, scooped out his cum, and brushed it low around my neck. Repeating it with the cum from my nose, he pulled back and got off the bed. I watched his pert butt, as he headed to the bathroom.

A moment later, he was back with a small hand mirror. He held it above me so I could see my face and shoulders.

"A pearl necklace for you," he said.

We laughed. "I'll have to leave it here with you or there will be questions," I said.

He nodded, and I got off the bed. In the bathroom, I washed off his cum, but, feeling a little wild and wondering, I was able to get in one lick of it from my lips.

***

"Where were you? You've been gone for over an hour!" Jody said, as I returned to our hotel room.

The wipes – damn, I left them in Tony's room. "Um, I saw Tony in the lobby. He had some asada French fries and invited me to his room."

She leaned forward. "*His room?* I can't wait to hear this story."

"We just shared the fries and talked. Nothing happened."

Jody rolled her eyes. "Right."

"What makes you think anything happened?"

"Because you're not wearing any makeup. You washed it off."

There was no getting anything by Jody, so I sat across from her. "Let's just say we got a chance to study the nudes."

Opportunity

We took in Ryan at the last minute because Hannah flaked out on us a week before we got the keys. I wasn't angry about having a male roommate – though this was supposed to be an apartment just for us girls in our last year of college – but then Madison got her dream internship in another city and also flaked out, and there we were, just Ryan and me. We had no luck finding someone to replace Madison, so each of us had to work an extra part-time job to afford the place, and with classes on top of that, we were exhausted.

Because of our schedules, about the only time we ever saw one another was while watching football on Sunday afternoons. It turned out that we both liked the Falcons, and so there we sat, on opposite ends of the couch, cheering every touchdown and groaning over as many fumbles.

By the last Sunday of October, a while had passed since I'd gone out, and I found myself glancing over at Ryan like he were some handsome devil across the nightclub. And I have to admit, Ryan was damn good looking. Sporting broad shoulders and a toned body, a perpetual stubble lined his strong jawline. His light blue eyes were killer. And that cute butt of his, so round and firm, perfectly filled out his jeans.

But each time I peeked his way, I just as quickly turned back, telling myself that getting involved with my roommate – who I barely knew – would just complicate matters. I mean, how could we be boyfriend-girlfriend when we could get together only one afternoon a week? A relationship like that couldn't work. And if we did anything but weren't dating, what would happen if I brought a guy back home some night? Would Ryan get mad, move out? Then I'd lose the place.

Oh, who was I kidding, I finally thought, when was I ever going to bring a guy home? I'd been too tired to party since moving into that apartment.

I refocused on the game. The Falcons had fallen behind early but kept it close, always a big play away from taking the lead. Jack Blazer, our quarterback, was off target just when the team would get going. He was known as a gunslinger, but the new coach forced him to play within a system where he checked receivers in sequence, and if none were open, he was to throw it away. Admittedly, it had cut down on his interceptions from last year, but they weren't winning by broad margins either.

"Blazer's so much better when they let him improvise," I said.

"Maybe," Ryan responded, his hair dark and wavy, black T-shirt hugging his well-muscled arms. "But he's got to play within the system, Jennifer, or his teammates won't trust him. They'll never know what he's going to do next."

Just then Blazer threw a long pass to his guy, who

caught it right on the sideline. We screamed "Yeahs!" and high-fived only for the referee to rule it incomplete because the receiver didn't get both feet down before going out of bounds.

"Oh no way!" I shouted at the same time Ryan hollered, "Are you blind, ref?" We looked at one another and shook our heads in disbelief.

Fortunately, the Falcons were able to snare a couple of hard-fought first downs and after a field goal got within a point. The momentum was swinging our way, and the players could feel it, too, as they'd slap the butt of the guy making a big play as running by him between downs. I have to admit, it was kind of a turn-on.

***

Despite being mad at Hannah and Madison, I missed them. I knew it didn't make sense, and so I did nothing about it. It's not like I had time to reach out anyway.

Then out of the blue one night, as I was falling asleep, Madison texted me.

How're you doing?

Alone and miserable and exhausted, I thought. At least Madison had a good reason to not take the apartment with me, so I responded, *Working a lot.*

Sorry. Madison knew she'd cast me aside. Then...*How is Ryan?*

Busy too. I yawned.

I met a guy. His name is Kaine. Super cute. Took me to the Bonavista, the restaurant that revolves.

Lucky you. *Great.*

A few moments passed before she replied. *We should*

get together when I'm back in town.

I pondered whether or not I wanted to. Then, before I could decide, I fell asleep, phone still in hand.

***

The Falcons got the ball back with less than two minutes to go in the game. Blazer drove them down ably, connecting with his receivers like the plays called for, but he also overthrew them a couple of times. With time running out, enough for maybe two plays, we still were not in field goal range. Blazer took the snap then suddenly protection broke down, and he scrambled. Locking eyes with a running back just a few yards away, Blazer pointed to a spot downfield then with a pass to that point hit him in stride. The back rushed down the field, weaving around defensive players for 10 yards then for 20, as we shouted him on. When he finally was taken down, close enough to try a long field goal, the Falcons called a time out with three seconds left on the clock.

The field goal team lined up. Ryan and I sat side by side, leaning forward together on the edge of the sofa, our hands clenched together in solidarity. The sandalwood scent of his aftershave filled my nostrils.

***

Madison never did text me back. I figured that was the end of it.

Then one morning I woke up to an email from Hannah. *Madison said you two weren't talking. I'm sorry about what happened. I feel that I'm the cause of it.*

Yeah, you sort of are, I thought.

When Austin asked me to move in with him, I didn't know what to do. But I love him and didn't want to cast any doubt in his mind about that.

So you abandoned us instead. Christ, Hannah, he was your boss.

We're engaged.

I didn't want to write something that sounded bitter. Yet if I was forgiving and we got together, I knew I'd only blow up at her.

So I went off to the shower to think about it. Then I went to class. By the end of the day, once home from work, I still hadn't responded.

The next morning, waking up tired from yet another night of not enough sleep, it slipped from my mind. With each passing day, not responding got easier.

***

For a few seconds, the kicker walked through his motions while a defensive player or two jumped up and down, warming up for a block. Then the two teams set, and the holder called for the ball. The center shot it back to him, and he placed it, as the kicker swung his leg forward. The ball sailed up over the defensive players' extended hands, and for what seemed like forever arced toward the posts until falling straight down the middle between the goal posts for the score.

We leaped up together, whooping and hollering – my body pulsed with joy, as it finally let loose – and we grabbed one another in a celebratory hug.

But when the moment came to pull away, we just stared for a long second into one another's eyes.

Our faces slowly moved closer to one another's, as if two merging clouds. He tilted his head slightly then stopped just before reaching my face and lightly grazed his lips over mine. The very tip of his tongue ran gently over my lower lip, and I opened my mouth a bit more. Suddenly his sweet tongue swirled in my mouth, as we pressed tighter against one another. The whole room spun. My arms slid around his neck to keep from falling over. I felt his growing erection, as our mouths pulled away for air. Something primal stirred deep within me.

My hands went to his shoulders, as I leaned in for another kiss. Through our jeans I ground my pussy against his hard cock. His woodsy scent wound around me, and I luxuriated in the warmth of crushing my breasts against a man's hard chest.

But then I pulled away, had to clear my head. What the hell was I thinking? "I'm sorry – I can't – we shouldn't do this."

He looked away then nodded quickly. "No, you're right. It would be...well..."

"Yeah, it would be."

He sighed deep. "I think I need a cold shower."

I grinned then looked away.

He traipsed off to his room and then the bathroom. A loneliness filled me, as I ached for human touch, for the warmth that says *you are important, you are worthy of love.* You don't get that serving tables or studying ancient history. God damn you, Hannah and Madison, for leaving me.

I glanced up at the wall clock to see what time it was,

and my eyes went big – not at how late it was but at the bathroom. Ryan had left the door open and had undressed. When he stepped into the shower, his round and perky butt flashed.

At the sound of the shower water, I stared at his silhouetted figure cleaning itself on the other side of the curtain. The mist of the hot water and the drops sliding down his arms softened his hard body. He brought both hands to his hair and rubbed in the shampoo. Even when not erect, he was well-endowed. I caressed my breasts.

The instant the shower water went off, my eyes shot back to the television screen, and my hands went under my butt. A moment or two passed, and he stepped out of the bathroom then stopped. I looked up at him.

His face shined red, as he held a white towel around his waist. "Oh damn – I always shower after you've left, and I didn't think about closing the–"

"It's okay," I cut him off, the heat of embarrassment covering my face as well. "I...uh...didn't see anything."

He suppressed a frown. "Oh. I'm going to change. Wanna watch the Lions game?"

I hated the Lions, the most inept team out there. "Um...sure."

He headed to his room, and I watched his cute butt, only partially covered by his towel, sway toward his room. My heart hammered faster, as a pressure built within my core.

I pointed the remote at the TV but paused. The on field reporter was interviewing Jack Blazer.

"I've got to give it to our guys," he said, his hair matted with sweat, "they really hung in there. When the opportunity presented itself, they came through. That's what this game is all about, taking hold of your opportunities."

He gave the sign of the cross, pointed to the sky, then trotted off.

I clicked the remote to the channel carrying the Lions game.

Oh fuck the Lions, I told myself; the only roar I want to hear was from a man cumming inside me after I'd fucked his dick long and hard. Time to pull a Jack Blazer.

I went down the hall and stood in his doorway, admiring the taut muscles of his backside, as he reached down to his bed for his T-shirt.

He turned around and, entirely naked, stumbled back. "Jennifer?"

With that, I walked straight up to him, dropped to my knees, and took his cock in my hand. Slowly my lips made their way over his cockhead, first up one side then the other, letting my hot breath and moist lips engulf part of him while the other was left in the dry cold anxiously waiting for my attention. He hardened instantly.

"Jennifer, we shouldn–"

Ignoring him, I grasped the base of his cock, slowly wrapped my lips around its head, then swirled the tip of my tongue just under his cockhead. Looking up at him with a mischievous glint in my eye, I licked the crown of his cock then kissed it. My free hand glided up his thigh and gripped it, the nails digging into the skin, as my lips wrapped about the cock. I tightened my grip on his shaft and then swallowed half of it. Slowly pulling away, I glanced up; his eyes were half shut and lips slightly parted, as if he were dizzy.

I'd won. Or rather something *inside me* had won.

As I took him in and out of my mouth, his large hand caressed the back of my head.

I kept the head of his cock in my mouth as my thumb and forefinger stroked down his shaft with little pressure and then back up, squeezing as I went. His breathing grew heavier, and his earthy scent rose as sweat beaded on him. I softly caressed his balls while my mouth bobbed up and down on his cock. The saltiness of his precum covered my tongue.

I pulled my head away from his cock, and he placed his hands beneath my underarms and lifted me to my feet. As his hard cock grazed my jeans, he slowly rolled my shirt up, exposing the waist, then over my head and somewhere into the corner of his room it went.

When both hands found and caressed my breasts, his fingers pinched my right nipple. I let out a soft moan.

I reached behind my back, unlatched the bra, and shrugged the straps off my shoulders. As my breasts fell free, he circled his tongue about them until reaching and flicking, several times, each nipple. My knees weakened and eyes closed.

As he worked on each nipple, his hands unsnapped my jeans and tugged them down past my ankles. I stepped out of them.

Then, holding the small of my back with his large hand, Ryan kissed up the side of my neck until reaching my ear. He whispered, "I've wanted you since we first met two months ago."

I pulled away, and as turning around, latched my thumbs inside the top band of my panties, pushing down first one side, revealing my crack and a butt cheek, then the other side so my ass was fully exposed. I left the panties at my thighs, bunched into a thin, vulnerable line. I've wanted him that long too.

Ryan placed an arm around me and with one hand kneaded my breast. As he gently pinched the nipple, his other hand palmed a butt cheek. My eyes closed, my breathing deepened, my knees barely held me up, as he glided me around, almost as if in a dance, so I faced the bed.

He stood behind me, his hard cock pressed against the crack of my ass, one hand squeezing a breast with a nipple between two fingers. "You are perfect," he whispered in my ear.

His hand gently pressed my back, pushing me downward so I stood bent over, tummy on the mattress. Then he dropped to his knees.

His thumbs pressed my ass cheeks just above my butthole, then the fingers reached to where my inner thighs met the bed, and he caressed upward, pinching my labia until the fingertips reached just below his thumbs. With each stroke, as his fingers reached my ass, my released labia unfurled farther until my moistness dripped upon his hand and my swollen clit protruded from its opening. Breathing hard, I wiggled, trying to brush my clit against him.

Then he thrust two fingers into my pussy while a finger of his other hand rested on my butthole; I dared not move lest it slip inside. I gasped with each thrusts, which only encouraged him to quicken his pace. I sank into the pleasure, hips rocking with the motion. OK, I thought, I may need to write Hannah and Madison thank you cards.

My hands grasped the sheets while my pussy arched up to meet his fingers. The bottom half of my legs tensing with each thrust. Then my ass tightened as my whole lower body squirmed. I bit down hard on the sheet.

A ticklish, hot wave rose from the center of my pussy and rippled out toward my fingertips and toes.

Ryan stopped thrusting, let me enjoy the moment. Then he stood. His hands gripped my waist, as his cock sat at my pussy's entrance. In a sports announcer voice, Ryan said, "He steps up under center, ready to take the snatch."

I broke out laughing.

Then he eased into me, and I gasped in pleasure. My hips rose to greet him. Pushing a little more, he slowly slid further inside me, inch by inch.

He paused as we relished the sensation of my body sheathing him.

I wondered why we hadn't done this a month ago when the Falcons won their first game.

A final thrust pushed him to the hilt.

With agonizing slowness, he drew his cock back then pressed in again, allowing his large member to stretch me with intense pleasure. My hips met his. Each time I tried to increase the pace, he backed off, leaving me almost empty.

After three failed attempts, I realized what he wanted.

Ryan swept his hand across his glorious cock, only its head in my entrance, then swiped my pussy juices down the crack of my ass. His wet finger rimmed my nether hole.

I moaned as my neck arched up.

Then his finger pressed into the hole. My ass tightened, and his free hand firmly pulled a butt cheek away from the other. His finger pushed until it was knuckle deep. My hips gyrated on his finger until it was all the way in, and then he thrust his cock fully inside me.

The walls of my pussy contracted around his cock, as some fantastical energy pent up inside rose in me like a wave, and then I let go, let that suddenly very real energy sweep over me.

He grunted loudly, as if in triumph, as I felt his warm seed fill me.

In the same instant, a second wave swept through me, and my body collapsed against the bed and trembled.

Ryan withdrew and climbed onto the mattress, his muscled body clad only in sweat, then offered his hands to help me climb up. I took them and rested my head on his chest, the curves of my body hugging his. My heart slowed and muscles relaxed, as placing a hand on his broad chest. He lay stretched out, his broad shoulders and chest angling to a narrow waist then widening to well-hewn legs, his spent cock only half-erect but still beautiful.

My head tilted back. His light blue eyes peacefully stared at the ceiling.

As his fingers gently stroked my hair, I looked him in the eyes. "I didn't know you felt this way about me."

"Haven't you seen the way I've been looking at you these past nine weeks?" he said.

"I guess I've been too tired to notice."

He nodded. "Maybe I've been too tired to do more than look."

"Are you tired now?"

He shook his head.

I grinned then crawled on top of him, rubbing my wet slit against his cock, hardening it. "Good. Because the second quarter is about to begin."

Vile and Foul

"I've done vile things...foul things."

"She did! Give her a good spanking," Kasie shouts, as she raises her glass of wine at the TV.

"Yeah, take her right over your knee," I add, and we laugh. Porn can be so stupid even when it's supposedly made for women.

Not that we care. We're two-and-half sheets to the wind, and by the time our wine glasses are empty, we should be a full three sheets.

The muscular man on the screen grabs the "vile" woman's hair, pulls her to the bed and as he sits on the mattress drags her over his lap. His free hand slaps one ass cheek then the next. Her fake wails are so loud, I wonder if they dubbed in the slapping sounds.

"Jillian, have you ever been spanked before?" Kasie says to me, her red hair brilliant as the afternoon sunlight shines through the window.

"During hazing week to get into Sigma." Brow furrowed, I look at her. "You were there, don't you remember?"

"No, I mean by a guy. During sex."

The man on the TV has stopped spanking the woman and switched to finger fucking her while she's still on his lap. Her moans grow in volume, hardly matching the thrusts of his finger.

"No," I say softly. "You?"

She shakes her head, takes another sip. At the rate we're going, we'll be asleep before dinner.

The man on the screen has gone back to slapping the woman's ass cheeks, turning them red, so he must be actually making contact. Most women in her position would be screaming and crying by then, but she's squealing with pleasure. Maybe they anesthetized her ass before filming.

"I'm sure a lot of guys wanted to spank us," Kasie says suddenly. "We were quite the teases."

"We still are."

"Damn right!" Kasie says, and we drink to that.

She's right. Neither one of us has changed much. Other than some crow's feet and having to spend a little more time at the gym to keep the weight off, we're still the slender, pretty-faced brunette and redhead that we were back in college.

The man on the TV has pulled the woman off his lap and bent her over the bed. He enters in one quick thrust and, gripping her waist, fucks her fast and hard from the start. She groans with every jackhammering thrust.

"You ever miss those days?" I say after a bit.

"All the time," Kasie says without hesitation. "Men our age are desperate to get married. They feel like they're falling behind."

I nod. "Fuck them once and they think we're engaged."

"That was the nice thing about young studs. All they wanted to do was fuck." She sips her wine then motions with her glass toward the TV. "You know, I think *he's* the one doing some vile and foul things to her right now."

The man on the screen pulls the woman's hair back, as he rams into her. A finger on his free hand is planted firmly in her butthole. He's calling her "a dirty slut" and "my little whore," as she continues to squeal in delight.

"She deserved it," I say, and we laugh again. "I'm glad you came down for the weekend, Kasie. It's great seeing you again. I haven't laughed like this in a while."

"Me either. I'm glad we're still friends."

"Once a Sigma," I start, and she finishes our sorority's unofficial motto with me, "always a Sigma."

A leaf blower starts up, and its roar drowns out the woman's fake squeals on the TV. A young man just as muscular as the guy on the screen walks past the living room window, taking care of my patch of Ohio's fallen autumn leaves. His dirty blond hair is apparent even under his baseball cap, as are those deep, chocolate brown eyes.

Kasie perks up. "Aren't you the lucky one? Who's that?"

"I see you've noticed Max. He's quite the hunk, isn't he?"

"For sure. Have you fucked him yet?"

I laugh. "Unfortunately not. He's my best friend Aime's son."

Kasie's full lips' pouted. "That's too bad. So your pal Aime lives next door?"

"Mm-hmm. She's gone for the weekend or I'd introduce you. Max is a student over at Ohio State, runs a yard business on weekends to pay the tuition."

"This Aime is gone, you say? Maybe some of Max's friends will come over later."

I laugh. "You're insufferable."

"But satisfied. Well, most of the time..."

We giggle, as I refill her glass of wine. "You know that guy on the porn video looks a lot like Bryant from college."

Kasie leans forward. "He does now that you mention it! Do you think that's him?"

I shake my head. "Bryant's dick was a lot smaller."

Kasie focuses on the screen as the guy's cock darts in and out of the fake screaming woman. "Yeah, it was."

There's a knock on the door. I jump up, fumble for the remote, see Kasie has it.

"Quick, turn it off!" I say.

She takes her sweet time picking up the remote, and as she does, I glance at the door. It's Max, looking through the window directly at us.

"Hurry up!"

Once the TV goes off, I speed walk to the door, open it. "Max, how are you?" A rush of cold air sweeps into the house. "Come in, warm up a little."

As I pull the door fully open for him, he steps inside, rubs his gloved hands and shivers a minute. He glances toward the TV and Kasie, who's looking around the chair at him.

"Hi, I'm Kasie," she says, giving him a smile and a

little wave.

He nods to her then looks at me. "I just wanted to see if you'd given any thought to signing up for the snow removal service?" His voice possesses a deep timbre.

I don't have the heart to tell him that in this poor economy I'm cutting back on expenses, and his service is one of those I probably can do without.

As if sensing my anxiety, Kasie quick speaks up. "Come sit down, Max. Looks like you've been working hard out there and need a rest."

His face reddens a little. "It's nothing too difficult–"

Kasie gives him that same pouty face no guy in college could resist.

"Well, I suppose a few minutes wouldn't hurt."

A broad smile returns to Kasie's face, and she pats the sofa cushion next to her chair. Max makes his way toward the living room, but I grab his wrist. "Your jacket and cap."

"Oh sorry," he says, and takes them off then places them and his dirty gloves on the coat hooks next to the door. "Wouldn't want to get leaves all over your house."

He heads into the living room, wearing a keen plaid flannel shirt and tight jeans, and I admire his pert ass. He sits down on the sofa right where Kasie patted.

"Jillian tells me you're going to OSU?"

He nods. "Studying business management."

"Impressive. Looks like you're putting what you've learned into practice."

I can tell what Kasie is up to; I've seen it a dozen times in college. Trying not stumble, I head to the kitchen for another wine glass.

"Attending school while running a business – that must be stressful," I overhear Kasie say from the living room.

Then the thought crosses my mind, *Can I do this with my best friend's son?*

Well, he's an adult; he can make his own decisions. Right?

I return to the living room with the glass and pick up the almost empty bottle of wine. "Drink?" I say to Max.

"I probably shouldn't, given that I'm operating equipment."

Kasie's seductions always calls for the guy to get a little drunk. Maybe he'll save me from having to make a decision. I set down the glass and bottle on the end table.

"Tell me more about this snow removal service," Kasie says.

Max goes into a long spiel about the services he'll offer and his low rates and what he plans to do with the money, all while Kasie gazes at him, smiling, pretending to listen intently.

When he finishes, she looks past him to me, "That sounds like a great service, Jillian. You should sign up."

"Well..."

They're both staring at me, waiting for me to say *yes* – Max because he obviously wants the money, Kasie because she probably wants to see more of Max. Who wouldn't? He's always got that sexy one day-old stubble on his face.

"Well," I repeat, "I'm probably not going to be able to, Max. With the economy as it is, I need to cut back on some of my expenses. I'm sorry, I wish I could."

He momentarily frowns. "No need to apologize, I understand."

Kasie leans toward Max, taps his wrist. "Oh, you're not giving up that easily, are you?"

Max's brow furrows. "Well, she's a neighbor and friend. It wouldn't be right to pressure someone into buying something from you just because they're your neighbor and friend."

"I admire your ethics," Kasie says. "But there must some kind of...*arrangement* that could be worked out."

His lips purse in thought for a long second. "Sure, that's possible. What do you have in mind?"

I sit there not saying anything, just staring at his chocolate brown eyes. If Kasie wants to seduce him, she can, but I'm not going to. "Um, well what would you suggest, Max?" I say.

"Maybe a discounted price. Or you could pay a set amount each month so that your payments extend into spring. Or-"

Kasie touches his elbow. "Oh Max, you're thinking of an arrangement in terms of *money*. Think outside the box. There are *other* ways of payment than the dollar."

Max's brow furrows again. I slowly shake my head, mouth *no* to Kasie.

"You'll have to ask Jillian what she has in mind," she says.

Max turns to me, those brown eyes of his

questioning. Kasie slowly nods, mouths *yes* to me.

"Well, let me think about it," I say.

Max rises. "That's no problem. I better get back to the leaf blowing."

"Are you sure you don't want to stay a little longer?" Kasie says. "We were just watching a video, and you could watch it a while with us."

My eyes go wide.

"Thank you anyway," Max says. "But it'll be dark soon."

"Okay then," Kasie says. "It was nice meeting you, Max." She bats her eyes at him.

"You too," he says and heads toward the door.

Kasie raises the remote and turns on the video. The woman's long moans and the man's grunts echo through the living room, as he thrusts into her pussy, his finger still fully buried in her ass.

Max turns around, stares with wide eyes at the TV.

Kasie and I look around the side of our chairs at him. Max blushes, as his eyes stay glued to the screen.

"You're not embarrassed by that are you?" Kasie nodded at the screen.

"Uh, no, I...uh, my apologies for interrupting you."

"Oh, you're not interrupting. Actually, you were about to *join* us."

"Well, the leaves *are* off the walkway and driveway." Max watches the screen the entire time he speaks.

I glance back at it. The man has finished pummeling the woman's pussy and is now working on pressing his cock into her ass. With each small push, she lets out a surprise yelp and then giggle.

Kasie speaks in her best sultry voice. "You finding this interesting?"

He gives an unconvincing shrug. His staring eyes tell the truth though. So does the hardening cock in his pants.

Kasie sits on the couch where Max had been and pats the cushion next to her. "You're welcome to watch. I bet you're wondering how it's all going to turn out."

I shoot Kasie a surprised look and mouth *stop*.

Kasie pretends like she didn't hear me. That was half the fun of being her friend – she drags you along into something you want to do but never would on your own.

"Okay," Max says, and he sits down beside Kasie, his body a little wooden, as if nervous.

Kasie looks at me. "I think Max wants something to drink."

I fill his glass, and as handing it to him, Kasie nudges her head toward the empty sofa cushion. Sitting there, I turn back to the screen.

The man has his cock about half-way in the woman's ass, and this time she is honestly feeling it, letting out grunts and groans, as she grips the sheets not so much out of pleasure but as if in pain and holding on for dear life.

Kasie watches the video for a few seconds then glances at Max's lap. She grins, and I look there too. His hardon presses his pants outward, like a long steel tube is in there.

Max notices us and pink-faced suddenly crosses his legs.

Kasie rubs his knee. "Oh, there's no need to be all embarrassed." She gently separates his crossed legs then runs a finger up his inner thigh and palms his bulge. "I wouldn't mind helping you with that."

He gazes at Kasie, as her fingers rub his cock through his jeans. He lets go a low moan.

I run a finger along my lips, found myself sucking on it. *Kasie already has taken this past the point of return,* I tell myself. *So long as he doesn't tell his mother, what happens with Sigma stays with Sigma.* I reach over and rub my hand on his chest, letting the fingers creep into the spaces between his shirt's buttons until I find skin.

Kasie undoes his jeans snap and pulls down his zipper, as my finger runs down the length of Max's torso then hooks inside his jeans and underwear and tugs at them. Kasie does the same on the other side, and Max lifts his butt so we can pull them down.

His long, thick cock bounces free.

Kasie smiles joyfully at it. "That's really fucking impressive."

Maybe it is the alcohol, maybe it is my lust, but I'm too far gone. "We should taste it," I say.

Kasie's head ducks into his lap, and she drags her tongue over his shaft. An instant later, she sucks on it as stroking its base with her tender fingers.

A deep moan escapes Max's mouth, and I take his chin in my hand then press my lips to his. He opens his mouth to me, and I stroke his tongue with mine.

I undo each of his shirt's buttons and kiss the revealed skin beneath, as Kasie slurps on his cock, her red hair splayed over his lap.

Once I reach the last button, Kasie comes up for air. I lean over then cup Max's balls and suck on each one. Kasie's head returns to bobbing up and down on his cock.

Max's moans of pleasure fill the room. His hand runs along my waist and caresses my ass. My pussy tingles.

Kassie pulls away from Max's cock and begins a striptease, first slinking out of her light sweater and then slowly removing the bra beneath.. Not that Max notices, for my hand takes over where Kasie's mouth left off, stroking his cock, it lined thick with her saliva. As she turns around and wiggles out of her tight jeans, his eyes close and head arches back.

When Kasie finishes undressing, I can't help myself. Her strawberry blonde patch always fires the lust inside me, and I leave Max's cock, get on all fours in front of Kasie, and run my tongue across her inner thigh. As she gasps in pleasure, my tongue finds her wet, swollen slit and darts inside.

Max must feel left out, for he gets on his knees behind me and undoes my jeans snap then tugs them downward along with my panties. I wiggle a little to help him slide them over my round ass then lift each knee in turn as he finishes pulling them over my feet.

He caresses my bare ass then gets on all fours behind me and swipes his tongue over my pussy. I gasp. When he pulls away, I wiggle my butt at him.

Kasie lays on the floor before me. I lean onto my elbows so my tongue can reach her patch, jutting my ass upward so Max can better reach it. He places both hands on my ass cheeks and spreads them until my pussy is fully exposed to him.

His tongue licks straight up my slit, separating the wet folds, and I gasp again in pleasure. Within seconds, his tongue finds my clit, and as my eyes close, my breathing deepens. He's right on target – must have had some practice with those freshmen girls at OSU – and soon my hips are gyrating into his face. One of my palms reaches back to his hand that holds my thigh, as my gasps turn into low moans that grow louder by the second.

I can't concentrate anymore on Kasie's pussy, and within seconds of me leaving it, her hand reaches up to the crown of my head and presses it to her slit. Though trying to flick my tongue against her clit, all I can do is gasp warm breath onto it, as my muscles tense.

"Right there," I manage to get out to Max. "Yes, yes, yes!"

My entire body tenses, then my hips buck into him, as I go cross-eyed with pleasure. A long second later, my body loosens, seems to half-melt onto my living room floor.

I roll next to Kasie and look up at Max, who's on his knees, his thick and long cock fully erect, as he stares down at two wet, naked pussies, probably not sure which one to fuck first.

"Did you like how I tasted?" I ask him.

He nods vigorously.

Kasie deserves a good orgasm for ensuring I got one, and I need time to rest before we get down to fucking, so I nod my head toward her. "If you liked me, then you've got to taste her strawberry shortcake pussy."

Max lays down on his tummy between her legs, places his hands on her thighs, and goes to work eating her out.

Kasie's neck arches back, and her hips slowly press into Max's face, as she lets go a low "Ohhhh."

Maybe Max's tongue is tired, for he keeps coming up for air, breaking the steady rhythm a woman needs to cum. So I get onto my tummy next to him and with a palm on the back of his head, hold it in place so he can't leave her pussy. He doesn't seem to mind, and within moments Kasie is moaning loudly.

Her entire body writhes, like it's under the spell of some witchdoctor. Max's hard body contrasts with her curves, and he remains focused on pleasing her. Watching two people make love in real life is far more exciting than watching two people act it out on TV.

Then Kasie's entire body shakes as she moans, the upper half of body folding forward then falling back onto the carpet with a smile of intense satisfaction. When her body stops twitching, I lift my hand from Max's head.

He gets on his knees, his mouth wet from Kasie's juices, and breathing hard. "That was a nasty thing you did, holding my head down between her legs," he says to me.

I grin. "Yeah, it was *vile*. So what're you going to do about it?"

"Lay on your back," he says.

I do, and before looking up at Max, he's on his knees between my legs, gripping my ankles and pulling my legs and ass into the air. His cock slides all the way into me, not giving me a chance to get used to his length or thickness, but I'm wet enough to accommodate him. Such is the pleasure of a young buck servicing you.

My breathing grows heavy, as Max pounds into me, and then Kasie gets on all fours over me and lowers her breasts to my mouth. I lick each one, swirling my tongue toward her nipples, and soon the room is filled with the sounds of Max's grunts, Kacie's moans, and my gasps.

Kasie looks up at Max, her nipple still in my mouth. "You've been fantasizing about her for a long time, haven't you?"

Max nods, his eyes half-closed as he thrusts, somehow gets out an "Yes."

"When you were a teenager, you jerked off thinking about her, didn't you?"

He nods again. "Yes."

"How foul! Well, this is your reward for taking good care of your body. See, good things do come to those who work hard."

As Max's grip tightens on my ankles and his cock hammers me even faster, Kacie shimmies down to my pussy. Her tongue darts out, somehow finding my clit.

"Oh fuck!" I let out, as the pleasure grows even more intense.

Max pulls out of me and thrusts his cock at Kasie face. She leaves my pussy and sucks on his member again, taking it deep into her mouth. The emptiness in my pussy, the coldness on my clit, is excruciating.

Then, as if sensing I needed attention, Max's cock fills me once again, and Kasie's warm tongue returns to my clit. I'm too dizzy to know anymore where the pleasure is coming from, and my body tenses.

Then Max brings my foot to his mouth, licks my toes as thrusting into me. It's too much, and my senses spill over the edge into orgasm. As I scream out in pleasure, Max's hot cum spills into me.

A few seconds later, we separate, our bodies slick with sweat, each of us gasping for air and the TV the only sounds.

"Will you ever do foul things again?" the man says to the woman, his cum splattered across her face.

"No sir," she says demurely, then – as the camera zooms in on her – she turns to the audience and winks.

All of us laugh.

"Looks like we missed the video," Max said.

Kacie grabs the remote and shuts off the TV. "We'll have to watch it again tomorrow."

I sit up. "Since your mother is gone, Max, you're welcome to spend the night with us." I deserve a spanking for the vile and foul thing I've done, after all.

"I'd like that," he says, his cock starting to deflate, though it's large even in its natural state.

"Oh, and you can't ever tell your mother about this, understood?"

His young face grins. "Sons never talk about their sex lives to their mothers."

Why didn't I think about that? "And about the snow removal service? We were thinking this might serve as payment for it."

Max shakes his head. "That only covered half of the season."

Kacie and I look at one another wide-eyed.

"But if you want to cover the other half of the season..." He taps Kasie's chest. "Then get on your back and spread your legs."

"Sure, anything to help a friend in need," Kasie says.

She rolls over, and Max gets on his knees between her legs and lifts them in the air as his now erect cock aims for her pussy.

She smirks. "Plow me, baby, plow me."

If you got a little excited from reading this book, please take a few moments to write a review of it.

amazon.com/review/create-review/?channel=glance-detail&asin=1948872692&ie

XOXOXO – Emily

Interview with Emily

Q: How did you come to write this collection?
A: I have a list of types of men that women generally find sexy – firemen, doctors, billionaire CEOS, etc. – and *young studs* was on the list. Several of my stories contain main characters who fit that category, so here we are. But the stories are less about young studs than the women protagonists and how they relate emotionally to these young, albeit muscular, men.

Q: Why young stud stories and not some other age?
A: I think it's a feature of my age. That age group of men is who I've mainly had sex with, yet as I enter my thirties I find myself "outgrowing" that age group. In some ways, these pieces are a personal reflection of what it means to have sex with a young man.

Q: Did you write the stories in the order they appear?
A: No. I arranged them so the opening pieces are in-depth explorations of women's sexual relationship with younger men then drilled down on specific topics. "Opportunity" was the first story in this collection that I wrote while "Vile and Foul" was the last.

Q: Which story was the most difficult to write?
A: "Bit of Pink" took the longest and required the most revising. There was a lot that I needed to get right in the

chronology of events. There's also a lot going on in the piece in terms of symbolism.

Q: Do you have a favorite from the collection?
A: Definitely "Bit of Pink." Leandra could be an actual, real person. She's a three-dimensional character who significantly changes.

Q: How long does it usually take you to write each of your short stories?
A: About 1-2 weeks. Some have come in a single afternoon, most need some gestation and revising.

Q: Do you ever run into someone who says, "You write WHAT?"
A: Sometimes, lol. I explain to them that good erotica is about the human heart and discovering one's sexuality. The Victorians among them still think it's porn, though.

Q: Is there anything you find particularly challenging when writing?
A: Ensuring I don't sound the same from story to story when describing sexual acts. To avoid that, I talk with a lot of women about their unique sexual experiences.

Q: Will you write more young stud stories?
A: Most definitely. I'm next going to return to another spanking anthology, though, and then after that maybe write an anthology of erotica stories set in a specific place, probably Los Angeles.

About Emily Rooks

Emily Rooks is the author of erotic romance that sizzles with passion and tension. Her stories explore sexuality from a woman's perspective and feature strong female protagonists. She holds a bachelor's degree in literature and creative writing and resides in Los Angeles.

True Lust Titles

Anthologies
- Backdoor Tales
- Spanking Tales
- Spanking Tales, Volume II
- Young Studs

Short Stort Standalones
- Atonement
- Chalk
- Opportunity
- Star Pupil
- Supergirl
- Venus Fly Trap

Better Sex Guidebooks
- Essential Foreplay Tips

Connect with Emily

BlueSky
emilyrookstruelust.bsky.social

Facebook
(limited posts)
facebook.com/EmilyRooksTrueLust

Goodreads
goodreads.com/user/show/146421357-emily-rooks

Literotica
literotica.com/authors/EmilyRooks/works/stories

Pinterest
pinterest.com/emilyrookstruelust

Website
emilyrookstruelust.com

X/Twitter
x.com/EmilyRooksTrueL